Tanner's Forever

Samson Boys: Book 2

Stephanie Renee

Chapter One

"When's Dad supposed to be here?" Alex, my eight-year-old asks.

I glance at my watch. "Twenty minutes, so you need to make sure your bag is packed. You know how much your daddy hates it when you forget something, and he has to come back."

"Already done. And I'm sure I didn't forget anything!" He exclaims before running out of the room.

"Check anyway!" I call after him.

I applaud his confidence, but I make a mental note to check his bag before he leaves. Last time one of the kids forgot something, my ex-husband, Judd, somehow found a way to blame me. He somehow finds a way to blame *everything* on me. He loves to remind me that I won't be winning any Mother of the Year awards anytime soon.

That's alright. He can keep his awards and kind words. I got the kids, and that's all that matters to me. For their sake, I will put up with any and all of the not-so-subtle digs that Judd throws at me.

As I fold another towel, our three-year-old, Joey, comes running into the room. "Momma!"

"Yes, darlin'?"

"Whatcha doin'?"

"Folding laundry," I reply, trying to hide my sarcasm at stating the obvious. "Are you excited about going to your daddy's?"

He smiles and nods. "He said we're going to race go karts!"

Of course he did.

Every time Judd has the kids, he makes sure to take them out to do something fun that I likely can't afford. It's his way of trying to fight his way into the role of favorite parent.

At times, it breaks my heart that I can't always be the "fun" one, but I don't bring any of this up to my kids. I've always vowed not to talk crap about their dad in front of them. It's not fair to put them in the middle.

So, just like usual, I paint on my best fake smile and say, "That sounds fun! Do you think you're going to win?"

His grin is so big that he looks like he might bust. "Yeah!"

That smile quickly fades, though, as his face falls. "Momma, what are you going to do while we're gone?"

The way he worries about me melts my heart. Out of my three boys, Joey is my wild child. If he had been my first-born, I don't know that I would have had the energy to have more. But he has the biggest heart when it comes to those he loves.

My little Sour Patch Kid.

"Don't you worry about me, darlin'," I tell him. "I'll keep busy.

"But you'll be alone."

Way to remind me of that.

We go through this every time he goes to his dad's. Every other weekend, I have to explain to him that I don't mind some alone time and that I'll be just fine. Truth be told, I'm a mother of three boys; I relish a bit of alone time.

But tonight, I actually won't be alone. "Sweetie, tonight, I'm hanging out with Aunt Nancy and Aunt Gina."

Gina and Nancy are my best friends, and they're the best "aunts" my kids could ask for.

"What are you going to do?" He asks.

Not wanting to tell my three-year-old that my friends are taking me out to get rip-roaring drunk and sing karaoke, I try to think of something a bit tamer to tell him.

Right at the moment I open my mouth, my thirteen-year-old, Chris, yells from downstairs, "Dad's on his way!"

"Joey, you better go put your bags by the door," I tell him as he sprints out of the room.

I take a break from laundry and head downstairs to make sure they are all ready to go. The less time I have to spend with Judd, the better.

Chris sits by the door, playing on one of his handheld video games.

"Is your stuff all packed?" I ask.

All I get is a nod.

I'm not sure how much of his attitude is just being an obnoxious teenager and how much of it is him still mad about the divorce. It's been a year since our split was finalized, but we were separated for a while before that. I think Chris has always partially blamed me for not trying harder. Maybe I should defend myself and tell him that it was his dad who ultimately walked out on me. But what good would that do? Chris lived with two married parents for over ten years, and then, his whole life got turned upside-down. Why make that worse?

And putting him between his father and myself is never fair. One day, he will see the truth on his own.

Hopefully.

I grab the small pile of laundry that has somehow accumulated by the front door and carry it to the living room. Before I get too far, I hear Chris call my name.

Well, he *mumbles* my name.

"Yes?" I look back at him.

"Can I take this to my dad's?" He asks without looking up.

I know he's referring to his video game. "Chris, you already know the answer. It's the same as every other time you've asked me."

"I don't get what the big deal is."

The big deal is that I spent every spare cent I had to buy that game for him for his birthday. I don't want anything happening to it while he is over there. I sure as heck know Judd wouldn't offer to replace it.

Not wanting to have this conversation for the twentieth time, I give him a stern, "Christopher."

I get a heavy sigh and an eye roll, but he drops it.

A knock on the door causes Charlie, our three-legged Beagle, to let out a couple long howls. The second I open the door, though, he runs to the other side of the room to hide. My boys found Charlie out in front of our house after he was hit by a car. After trying like crazy to find his owners, the kids finally convinced me to keep the poor thing. I was hesitant at first, especially with the vet bills, but it didn't take me long to cave. He's been the best boy ever since. To anyone that's not us, though, he's extremely skittish. Rightfully so.

I open the door enough for Judd to step through. Immediately, he looks me up and down, examining my ripped jeans, tie-dye shirt, and messy bun. He purses his lips in disapproval.

Crossing my arms over my chest, I ask, "Something you want to say, Judd?"

With an arrogant smirk, he replies, "Just wondering if it's laundry day."

The smug look on his face shows that he is way too proud of that jab.

"Judd, there are three boys living here. *Every* day is laundry day."

I think it's a witty comeback, but the way Judd's jaw clenches, I can tell that he doesn't think so. My stomach instantly forms into a knot, waiting for him to start spewing venom. That's what Judd does when he gets mad. A nervous fear washes over me as I prepare for the backlash.

Judd was never violent with me. I never worried about him putting his hands on me, but the psychological warfare he brought to the table was enough to give me ulcers for the final years of our marriage. I found myself willing to do anything to keep him happy so that I didn't have to endure all the insults and harsh words he would sling at me. After a while, though, nothing made him happy. He looked for excuses to get mad.

Not wanting to argue in front of the kids, I open my mouth to try to smooth things over, but the kids appear, all ready to go.

They each give me a hug and tell me they love me on their way out the door. Judd stands there, impatiently sighing.

How is it that this guy that used to be so head-over-heels in love with me turned out to be such a narcissistic jerk? He went from being crazy about me to hating everything that I was.

Thankfully, he doesn't linger once the kids are out the front door. But he feels the need to get in one final jab before he leaves. "For God's sake, Erin, take a shower. You look like hell."

I shut the door behind him and lean against it, trying to breathe through the panic that had begun to set in. I'm not even married to the man anymore, and I still let him get under my skin. I know I shouldn't, but a fifteen-year-long habit is a hard one to break.

Charlie comes shuffling across the room to me. When he reaches my feet, I sink to the floor so that he can crawl into my lap. I should probably get a couple of things done before Nancy and Gina get here, but everything can wait a few more minutes.

"Such a good boy," I tell him as I scratch behind his ears. "You and me—we are just a couple of broken souls, aren't we?"

"I can't believe you talked me into wearing this," I tell Gina across the table.

"Are you kidding? You look fucking hot," she replies, sucking the lime out of her margarita.

I look down at the lacy black top. "This shirt is missing the bottom half. My poochy belly pokes out, making me look like a certain honey-obsessed bear."

Nancy starts laughing so hard she chokes on her drink.

Gina holds up her fingers, ready to tick off the reasons why this outfit was a good idea. "One, you're wearing high-waisted jeans. No one can even see your belly. Two, those jeans make your ass look fantastic. And three, your tits are out of this world."

My eyes glance at my chest. The push-up bra that Gina picked out from the bottom of my drawer makes my large breasts look perkier than normal. As a woman who lives in t-shirts and leggings the majority of the time, this outfit is way out of my comfort zone.

My two best friends also talked me into wearing my hair down, putting on makeup, and rocking cowgirl boots.

Gina is always used to looking her best. With no kids and no serious relationships, she constantly looks like she's ready to have a night out on the town. And Nancy has one of those gorgeous, naturally pretty faces that looks good no matter what. It's obnoxious.

Between my full-time job, motherhood, and life in general, I'm usually the haggard-looking one of the bunch. I have to admit that sometimes, I feel a bit jealous of my friends. Not in a malicious way or even in a way that makes me wish my life was different. It was just hard watching them live their best lives in their twenties while I was up to my eyeballs in dirty diapers.

I love my kids, and I wouldn't trade them for anything. But before they came along, I wasn't even sure I wanted kids. I wanted to go to college and try my hand at writing books while I traveled the world. Then, a boy convinced me to settle down with him. I got three awesome kids out of the deal, so I don't want to complain. It was just rough being knee-deep in motherhood while my friends were climbing their career ladders during the day and adding notches to their bedposts at night.

Gina gets up to get us another round of margaritas while Nancy and I giggle at the girl on stage who is slurring the words to a popular Britney Spears song.

When she finishes, Nancy turns to me. After taking a sip of her drink, she asks, "So, how are you doing?"

Without even thinking about it, I sail into talking about the kids. I talk about how they've been and what they've been up to.

When I come up for air, she says, "Erin, you know I love those boys more than I love myself, but I asked how *you're* doing."

"Oh," I reply. "I'm okay, I guess."

"How are things with Judd?"

"Same, I guess. He still makes me a nervous wreck. At this point, I'm not sure if I'll ever get over it."

She sets her hand on top of mine. "You will. It will just take some time."

Another woman gets on the stage, ready to sing. Karaoke has never really been my thing. I've been told I have a nice voice, but that doesn't mean I want a room full of people to hear it. I figure tonight, I can probably get out of it because it's a mad house, and it looks like there's a long line.

But I'm about to find out that I'm not going to get that lucky. Gina shows back up at the table with three margaritas and a black binder.

She hands it to me and says, "Pick a song."

I try giving it back to her. "I don't think so, Gina. Looks like there's quite a few people in front of me."

"Sweet cheeks, I added our names to the list when we got here. Nancy and I are doing a duet next, and then, you're up."

I could argue, but Gina's stubbornness is legendary. There's no way I'd win the battle before it was time for me to sing. Instead, I start chugging my margarita for some liquid courage. I'm going to need it.

Chapter Two

TANNER

"Are you going to take your shot?" I ask my older brother, Devon, who has been holding his pool cue for the better part of two minutes.

"Why do I do this to myself? Why do I say yes to coming to play pool with you when I know you're going to wipe the floor with me?"

"Because it keeps you from sitting at home bored on a Friday night while your girl is out with her friends."

This is the first time in forever I've managed to drag Devon away from Kyra. She takes up almost all of his time, which wouldn't be an issue if she didn't treat him like something she stepped in. Even tonight, I know we are hanging out on borrowed time. Soon enough, she will call him, and he will go running off into the night.

He lines up his shot but misses everything on the table.

"Glad we aren't playing for money," he says with a heavy sigh.

Joking, I reply, "Wouldn't want to put my own brother in the poor house."

He laughs. "I appreciate that. Speaking of brothers, where's our oldest one at tonight?"

He sips his beer while I line up my shot. "He said he and Avery were having a date night."

Duke is the oldest of the Samson boys. He's a good fifteen years older than me, and he was in the Navy for half of his own life. We have just recently started getting closer. The military fucked up his head pretty good, but Avery, his girl, has slowly helped heal all of his invisible wounds.

Devon says, "I'm so glad that grumpy son of a bitch found someone who makes him smile."

"Yeah," I agree. "Avery is pretty great. We should all be so lucky to find someone like her."

He gives me a half snort. "Bro, in all those women you've been with, you can't find a decent one?"

"You make me sound like a man-whore."

"If the shoe fits."

I give him a hard punch to the shoulder. It's true that I've been with my fair share of women, but it's probably not as many as my brother thinks.

He pulls me out of my thoughts. "What about that one girl that you were dating? Amy?"

"Amber," I correct.

"Whatever."

"We wanted different things."

"Oh?"

I nod. "Yeah, I wanted to get serious. She wanted to date her academic advisor."

"Shit, man, that sucks."

"Yep. But you know what the worst part is? I wasn't even that upset about it."

"Guess that goes to show you that she wasn't the one," he says.

"I'm just tired of dating twenty-somethings."

His eyes narrow in on me. "You know that *you're* a twenty-something, right?"

"I'm aware. I'm just ready to find someone who cares about something more than what's on the outside. A woman who has some substance to her."

"You'll find her," he says, trying to be reassuring.

"I guess. It makes it hard with my schedule. For most women, every other weekend isn't near enough. They're either worried that I'm cheating, or they do it while I'm gone."

"You ever stepped out on a girl while you were on the road?" He asks.

"Nah, man. I'm a lot of things, but a cheater isn't one of them."

"You're a better man than most, Tanner. A lot of men would fill the loneliness while they were on the road."

"Look, if I'm single, that's one thing. I'm not opposed to having some fun, but if I have a girl waiting for me back home, I'm waiting until I can be with her. My hand will get me by if I get lonely enough."

My brothers and I all tend to live by a certain code when it comes to the fairer sex. We watched our mother get treated like crap when we were younger by every Tom, Dick, And Harry she could find. We watched every guy she dated—or married—make her cry. The three of us took the same silent vow to never make a woman cry like that.

I'm no saint. But I'm no cheater either.

Just a hopeless romantic looking for someone to share my life with.

Devon points to the stage. "Are you going to sing?"

"Do I look like I sing karaoke?"

"I don't know. With that hair, you might."

Both of my brothers love to give me shit about my hair. It's a little past my shoulders and blonde in color. I don't care what either of those fuckers think. Women love my hair.

I take my final shot on the pool table, securing my win against Devon.

Pointing to a couple of women stepping onto the stage, he asks, "Want to grab a table and enjoy the show?"

"Sure."

We walk over and sit at an empty table in front of the stage. I'm surprised one this close is open, but I guess no one wants to be this close to all the bad singing.

When we sit down, Devon's eyes immediately lock onto the women—the taller one in particular.

"Damn, look at the legs on her," he says.

Both of the women are cute, but neither of them really do it for me. Maybe I'm just not in the mood. They start singing a popular song. They can't carry a tune well, but they're having fun.

In the middle of their singing, Devon asks, "So, when do you get back on the road?"

"Monday."

"And you come back when?"

"Probably a week and a half or so. Right now, I'm home about every other weekend. Lord willing I get this supervisor position soon so that I can be home more."

The women finish up their song. Before they get off the stage, they pull a woman who I assume is their friend up there with them.

And this one catches my eye.

My lord, she's gorgeous.

Okay, it's definitely not that I'm not in the mood.

She has dark, straight hair, big blue eyes, and cute pouty lips.

And that body? Holy shit.

You ever hear that saying thick thighs save lives? I'm fairly sure this woman's thighs could bring me back from the dead. And she's got the juicy booty to match.

Even with her on the stage, I can see her cheeks turning pink as the bright spotlight hits her. Embarrassment shows as eyes start to fall on her. As the music starts, I worry she's going to chicken out and run off the stage. But right before the first verse starts, she grabs the mic and starts to sing.

And boy, can she sing.

The woman is belting out the words like it's some sort of American Idol audition. She sings the country song, Heads Carolina, Tails California which makes everyone go crazy and start cheering. Surprisingly, that seems to make her look even more embarrassed.

Devon starts telling me some story about Kyra, but I don't hear a word he says. All I can focus on is the woman on the stage. I have to meet her and maybe buy her a drink.

My eyes stay glued to her the entire performance. I anxiously wait for the song to end because as soon as it's over, I plan to go introduce myself.

Chapter Three

ERIN

"That was amazing!" Gina cries as I step off the stage. "And you didn't want to sing!"

"Thanks, but I think that's enough excitement for me for the night... or the foreseeable future."

There's already another margarita waiting for me back at the table. "Are you guys trying to get me drunk?"

Gina scoffs. "They're just margaritas."

Yeah, BIG margaritas.

I'm not the drinker that I used to be. Sure, I can down some wine when I'm at home, drinking while I get lost in a good book, but that's a lot different than a boatload of tequila—or as I like to call it, my bad decision juice.

As I sit down to start on the next one, I figure I should get some water too. Otherwise, tomorrow morning, I'll be too hungover to function. And I don't want to spend my entire weekend with a killer headache.

"Be right back," I tell my friends. "Need to hydrate."

I stand up on semi-wobbly legs and head toward the bar. While I wait for the bartender, I hear a deep voice next to me.

"That was quite the performance."

"Oh, thanks," I mutter, figuring he's just being nice.

"Mind if I buy you a drink?"

My eyes flick over and see an absolutely gorgeous man standing beside me. He's tall, blonde, and has a jawline that looks like it's cut from stone. I'd guess he's a good ten years younger than me.

Convinced there's no way he could be speaking to me, I look around.

He leans forward a little. "I'm talking to you."

Man, he smells good.

"Oh," I stammer. "Thanks, but I still have a margarita I need to finish. I just came to get a water."

"Well, how about when you finish your margarita?" He asks.

I still have no idea why he's talking to me. I'm not typically a woman that gets hit on—especially by someone who looks like this guy. His bad boy looks are enough to make good girls lose their wits.

"Maybe," I say, trying to keep my cool. "If I can still walk after I finish this one.

He smiles, and holy crap, it's gorgeous. And I catch a glimpse of something in his mouth.

Is that a tongue ring?

Oh man, if only fifteen-year-old me could see me now.

"Do you want to play some pool with me?" He asks, pulling me out of my thoughts.

I actually consider it a moment before remembering that I didn't come here alone.

"I would, but I'm here with a couple of my friends. I don't want to leave them hanging."

"Fair enough." Before he walks away, he leans in to whisper, "I'll be over at the tables if you change your mind.

I have no idea what just happened, and honestly, I wonder if all the tequila is playing tricks on me. Maybe instead of beer goggles, I have on margarita goggles.

Or maybe he really is as hot as I thought he was.

Finally, the bartender gets to me and hands me my water. I walk back to the table where both of my friends sit with their mouths hanging open.

"What?" I ask.

"Uhm, who was that?" Gina asks.

"I didn't get his name."

"Why the hell not? What did you talk about?"

I shrug my shoulders. "He asked if he could buy me a drink and then if I wanted to play pool with him."

Gina rolls her eyes and lets out a huff. "Then, why the fuck are you back here with us?"

"We are supposed to be having a girl's night. I didn't want to just bail."

"Sweetie, we are fine. I think I speak for the both of us when I say we are more than willing to take one for the team if it means your vagina comes out of retirement."

Shocked, I reply, "My vagina is not in retirement."

"Self-employment doesn't count."

"Ha-ha. Very funny. It's just on sabbatical. Besides, what's the point?"

Nancy chimes in now. "What do you mean?"

"I mean, it's not like anything can come from it. One, that guy looks way younger than me. Two, I have three kids. There's no way I have time for any of that. Plus, you know Judd and I have an agreement not to date anyone in front of our kids unless it's serious."

Gina stops me before I can go any further. "Whoa! You're not asking this guy to play stepdad to your kids. Hell, you're not even asking him to *meet* your kids. But maybe you can just have fun and let loose. You're wound way too tight. Remember, even Rapunzel was a prude until some guy pulled her hair the right way."

Nancy says, "Erin, you're a mom. You're not dead. When was the last time you had an orgasm that wasn't by your own fingers?"

I go to open my mouth, but Gina adds, "Or your vibrator!"

I think back, trying to remember the last time I had sex—even though the last time Judd made me come was way before that.

When I run out of fingers to count on, Gina stops me. "My point exactly."

Nancy says, "Look, all we are saying is have some fun. See what happens. If it's a dud, who cares? Eventually you will have to put yourself back out there. What better way to dip your toes back in the water than with an extremely hot guy?"

"I'm just a little out of my element here." I lean in to whisper, "He has a tongue ring."

Gina grins. "Girrllll, that's a *good* thing. Have you ever been eaten out by a guy with a tongue ring?"

Rolling my eyes, I reply, "I think you already know the answer to that."

"You need to," Gina says while Nancy nods.

For a few more minutes, my friends tell me all the reasons why they think this is a good idea. And you know what? Maybe it's the tequila, but they are actually making a lot of sense. As much as mom guilt is trying to hold me back, a little bit of fun may be exactly what I need.

I'm feeling the effects of the bad decision juice.

To keep it going, I chug down the rest of the margarita and tell my friends that I'm going for it. They both smile and wish me luck as I head over to the cluster of pool tables. They sit in one corner kind of away from everything else. You can still see the stage, but everything's a bit more secluded.

Butterflies swarm in my stomach as I wonder if he's even still over here—or if he's already hitting on someone new. Much to my surprise, when I spot him, he appears to be hitting balls by himself. He knocks in two and looks up at me.

There's that smile again.

"Hey, you," he says.

"Hi," I nervously reply.

He holds the pool cue in both hands, leaning against it. "I don't think I properly introduced myself. I'm Tanner."

"Erin," I say in return.

"Did you change your mind about pool?"

I nod. "I figure I could use a little fun, but I haven't played much pool."

"Eh, me either," he says, but I don't believe him.

He walks over and sets up the balls in that triangle thing. He asks, "Your friends didn't get mad that you came over here?"

"No, they encouraged it."

He grins. "Remind me to thank them."

As he looks at me, I can see Tanner's eyes are the most crystal shade of blue I've ever seen. I've always been a sucker for blue eyes.

Tanner walks over and grabs a second pool cue and hands it to me. "Do you want to break?"

"Nah, I'm good. Go for it."

A waitress walks by and stops to ask Tanner if he needs anything. She acts like I'm not even there.

Thankfully, Tanner doesn't follow suit. He looks at me. "Are you ready for another margarita?"

I should probably say no, but at this point, I'm on a roll.

"Sure."

He tells the waitress and orders himself a beer before handing her a twenty and telling her to keep the change.

As he hits the balls on the table, they go flying in different directions. A couple fall in the corner pockets.

When it's my turn, I step up to take my own shot, and of course, I hit nothing.

Not surprising.

When my next shot ends up the same way, Tanner walks behind me. "Can I help?"

"Please," I giggle. "But I warn you I don't know that there's any help for me."

"Line up your shot," he tells me. "But don't actually hit anything yet."

I do as he instructions and wait for him to tell me what's next, but when I feel his hands touch my arms, I realize he intends to *show* me instead.

One of his hands repositions my arm while the other moves to my hip.

"Lean forward," he says in a low voice.

I swallow the lump in my throat as I bend over so the top half of me is parallel to the table. I can't help but notice my ass is pressing into Tanner's groin. Trying to see if I can feel what he's packing, I wiggle around a little bit.

What the hell am I doing?

I try to play it off like I'm just repositioning, but apparently, I'm not fooling anyone.

I feel him lean over me. Goosebumps cover my skin as he whispers, "If you want to see it, all you have to do is ask."

My breath hitches in my throat as I try to keep my composure.

He finishes helping me line up my shot, and with his hands guiding me the whole time, I manage to knock a ball in.

"Good job, beautiful," he says before standing up.

Immediately, I miss his hands touching me. Maybe the alcohol is hitting me a little harder than I thought because my mind is flashing with thoughts of going to bed with this guy.

After Tanner stands behind me to help me make another shot, I turn around to look at him.

"How old are you?" I ask, a little scared to know the answer.

"Twenty-five."

Hm. Not quite as young as I thought but still not great.

"Aren't you going to ask how old I am?" I ask as he lines up his own shot.

"Nope. My momma always taught me it was rude to ask a woman that question." He shoots me a wink.

"It doesn't bother you that I'm older than you?" I ask, glutton for punishment.

"Not even a little bit. Age is just a number."

Oh man, he's good. Deciding to jump on board, I'm going to see where this wild night takes me. Sipping my margarita that the waitress dropped off, I buckle up to enjoy the ride.

Chapter Four

TANNER

When I saw Erin coming to join me at the pool tables, I was pleasantly surprised. When she was shaking her ass on me while I was helping her with a shot, I was straight shocked.

Not only is she gorgeous, but she has a little naughtiness in her.

I like it.

As we take turns in pool, she asks, "So, do you just come here by yourself and hustle people in pool?"

I laugh. "My brother was here earlier, but his girlfriend called and wanted to meet up, so he left pretty quick. We just sometimes come here to blow off some steam. I just got back into town."

"Oh?"

"Yeah, I travel a lot for work. Usually, I'm gone for a week or two at a time."

"That must be hard," she says.

"Eh, it's not so bad. It makes me appreciate being home more."

"Sorry your brother ran out on you."

"It's alright. I think I got the better end of the deal," I tell her, and she gives me a cute smile.

As I take my next shot, I ask, "So, where'd you learn to sing like that?"

She shrugs her shoulders. "I was in choir in school, but since then, I just put on performances when I clean my house. Are you going to sing something?" She points to the stage.

"Oh, no, beautiful. No one needs to hear that."

"Are you chicken?" She jokes.

"Absolutely."

We both start laughing.

Erin tries to line up her next shot but is having trouble. I decide to shoot my own metaphorical shot, and I walk up behind her once again. As my hand rests on her hip, thoughts flash through my mind of grabbing onto these hips while I thrust into her. I'm trying not to be a pig, but fuck, it's hard. And if she keeps wiggling that ass, something else is going to get hard.

"Erin, are you trying to drive me crazy?"

She fakes innocence. "I don't know what you're talking about."

"Mm-hmm."

I feel her push back against me. Oh yeah, she knows *exactly* what she's doing.

Whispering in her ear, I ask, "Do you know how sexy your ass is?"

She shakes her head back and forth.

"Maybe later on, you'll let me show you."

I might be coming on a bit strong, but this woman has my head spinning. If she'll let me, I'd love to take her home and make her feel good all night long.

She said she was looking for some fun, and I'm sure I can show her that. Over and over again.

After she hits her shot, she turns around to face me. "Are you trying to seduce me, Fabio?"

The nickname makes me laugh. "Fabio?"

She nods. "Long blonde hair. Nice body. Looks like you belong on the cover of a romance book."

"Is my seducing you working?"

She thinks for a minute before holding up her finger and thumb with about an inch between them. "Maybe just a little. Do you want to make things more interesting?"

"How do you suppose we do that?"

"If you win this game of pool, I'll let you come home with me."

"Oh, beautiful, you've got yourself a deal."

Thinking I have this in the bag, I take my shot and knock in a ball. But I forget that Erin has one very effective secret weapon.

Her ass.

She bends over right when I'm about to shoot, and I don't hit a damn thing.

"Oh, you want to play dirty?" I ask. "Let's play."

When it's her turn, I walk up behind her. With one hand, I grab her hip and lean into her. Now, there's no doubt that she can feel my cock through my jeans.

The next five minutes are spent seeing who can distract the other one more.

She asks, "What do I get if I win?"

"Whatever you want."

She looks up at me, running her tongue over her bottom lip. "Anything?"

"Anything."

I expect her to say something dirty—to tell me some wild fantasy that she has. And I'm ready to give her absolutely anything she asks for.

"I want you to get up there and sing."

Okay, not what I was expecting.

But I'm still confident that I'm going to win. I only have one ball to knock in before the 8 ball.

"Deal."

I line up my shot and get ready to end this game right here and now, but Erin stands behind me, reaches around, and grazes the front of my jeans.

Man, she's fucking hot.

This woman is a complete mystery to me. She gives off a good girl vibe, yet she seems to have a streak of mischief. I can't believe that someone as fun and gorgeous as she is has ended up here alone.

When she gives me a light squeeze, I completely miss the shot I was about to take and hit the 8 ball instead. In slow motion, I watch it roll into the corner pocket.

She looks up at me with her pretty brown eyes. "I'm not an expert on pool, but I'm pretty sure that means I win, right?

Sighing, I ask, "What would you like me to sing?"

"You pick."

Okay, maybe I won't get in her pants, but at least I can make sure I make her smile.

Chapter Five

ERIN

The bad decision juice I've been guzzling all night may as well be a magic potion. It has managed to turn a shy, nervous woman into a huge flirt.

I. Grabbed. Tanner's. Dick.

In the middle of a bar.

But I have to admit it was nice.

Very nice.

Convinced, I was going to lose at pool, I was fully prepared to follow through and take Tanner home. The more he touched me, the more I wanted to go further.

Oh yeah. Tequila is magical.

But by some crazy miracle, I won the game. I thought about letting him off the hook and skipping straight to leaving. But honestly, I want to see him sing. He saw me sing earlier. It's only fair.

I walk over to the table where my friends were, but all that remains is a few empty margarita glasses.

I pull out my phone and see a text from Gina.

We decided to hit the road. Now, you have NO reason not to go home with the hottie. I expect a full report tomorrow. If you need us, call. We will be there in a heartbeat.

I should've known they'd bail.

Oh well. I'll give her hell for that later.

Right now, my attention is drawn to Tanner who is walking onto the stage. I'm surprised he didn't have to wait for a while for his turn. That smile of his probably gained him a couple spots in line.

I start cracking up when the speakers start to blare Pour Some Sugar on Me.

And although Tanner can't sing very well, he puts on a Grammy-worthy performance. A couple of cute, perky college co-eds sit at the table next to mine, and I can hear them talking about how hot Tanner is.

No shit, Sherlock.

Self-doubt washes over me. This gorgeous man is probably going to ditch me the second he sees these hotties bat their fake eyelashes at him.

But as Tanner belts out the lyrics, I notice something. No matter how much these girls try to get his attention, his eyes stay fixed on me the entire time. The look he gives me shows he's still interested.

When the song comes to an end, he walks off the stage, and the two girls try to stop him.

Immediately, their hands start running over his chest and shoulders. My stomach sinks as I wonder what they're saying.

But it doesn't matter.

Tanner grabs their hands and moves them off of him. He points to me before walking away. Both of them are quick to give me the dirtiest looks they can muster.

The petty side of me decides to give them something to really be mad about. I wrap my arms around Tanner's neck. Leaning up as far as I can, I'm thankful he meets me halfway so I can press my lips to his.

Holy crap.

I haven't kissed a guy besides Judd in close to fifteen years. And before that, it was just a couple of fellow highschoolers. I don't remember either of them kissing anything like this. Tanner and I aren't even using our tongues, and already, I'm itching for it to go further.

When I pull back, he smiles. "What was that for?"

"Figured I should at least kiss you before asking you if you want to go home with me."

Surprise washes over his features. "You ready to get out of here?"

"Do you have a car here? I didn't drive."

"I have my motorcycle."

Of course, you do.

I'm nervous he's going to ask me to ride it with him, but he says, "But I've been drinking more than I feel comfortable driving after. There are usually a couple cabs outside on karaoke night."

I let him lead the way out of the crowded bar into the Texas heat. Even when it's dark, Texas is still an oversized oven most of the time.

Two minutes later, we are in the back of a cab, heading to my house. I guess we could have gone to Tanner's place, but I'm already taking a chance by being alone with someone I barely know, so I'd rather be at my own house.

My fingers run and down his thigh, inching further toward his dick with each pass.

His lips brush against my ear as he whispers, "Do you really want to see who can tease who more?"

All I give in response is a squeeze to the base of his member through his pants. He lets out a deep breath and a barely audible groan.

The arm that's around my shoulders moves down so that his fingers dip below the fabric of my low-cut shirt. His touch on my skin sends electricity shooting through me.

I find myself holding my breath as he finds my nipple. He rolls it between his thumb and finger, and I try to stifle my moan. My clit pulses as I ache for more.

For all of it.

I look up at him as my breathing quickens. He uses his other hand to grab my chin and angle me toward him for a kiss. It starts slow, but it doesn't take long for my mouth to open for his tongue.

I turn my entire body toward him and grab his shirt, attempting to pull him closer to me. With me facing him, he uses both hands to palm my breasts through the thin material of my shirt.

I'm sure this cab driver is getting an eye-full, but right now, I couldn't care less. He's driving too dang slow. Time ticks by impossibly slowly as I resist the urge to whip Tanner's cock out right here and now.

His kiss is nothing but fire and passion, and I can't seem to get enough.

Thankfully, the car finally pulls up outside my house. Tanner pays, and we head up the walk.

Before I open the door, I hold up my finger. "Can I just have a minute?"

He looks beyond confused, and I expect a follow-up question, but it never comes. He just says, "Sure. Take your time."

"One second." I slip inside and quickly try to make sure there's a clear path to the bedroom. I'm doing my best to avoid having the whole "I have three kids" conversation. Seems like a mood killer. Thank goodness I've been too lazy to put up photos, so those won't give me away.

As fast as I can, I run up the stairs to my bedroom. I quickly toss the piles of clean laundry into my closet and light some candles. I don't intend on having the lights on and having him run in terror from my stretchmarks and C-section scar.

After taking one final look around, I mutter, "Good enough."

I rush back downstairs and tear open the front door. Thank goodness Tanner is still standing there... and looking sexier than ever. He smiles as I grab his hand and pull him inside. I waste no time in leading him right up the stairs.

When we get to the bedroom, I shut the door and immediately start to take off my clothes. Nervous excitement washes over me, making my hands shake in the process.

I don't get very far before Tanner grabs my arms. "Hey, beautiful. What's your hurry? I want to make this last a while."

As he pulls me in for another kiss, I don't say a word but instead melt against him. He runs his fingers through my hair as I get lost in the moment.

He pauses long enough to pull the shirt over my head. He looks down at my breasts which practically spill out of my lacy black bra.

In a whisper, he says, "Holy fuck, Erin. These are gorgeous."

He sinks to his knees in front of me, making him eye-level with *the girls.* He thumbs my nipples through the thin fabric. His hands reach behind me to unhook the clasp. Slowly, he drags the straps down my shoulders until it gently falls to the floor.

I wish my breasts didn't hang quite as low as they do, but Tanner doesn't seem to mind. He grabs one in each hand and sucks one nipple into his mouth. My head falls back as my fingers mess with his long hair.

I let out a loud moan as he flicks his tongue ring against the hard points.

"You are so fucking sexy," he whispers against me before moving his attention to the other nipple.

It's been years since I've been called sexy, and I could listen to Tanner say it all night long. I'm so turned on that I may come just from him playing with my nipples. But Tanner has other plans. After focusing a moment more on my chest, he moves onto the undoing the button on my jeans. As he pulls them down, I'm grateful that the candles don't provide much light. I doubt he can see my scars in the darkness.

But my stomach pooch is on full display. My hunky date doesn't seem to care, but I decide to try and distract him anyway. Reaching down, I pull his shirt over his head before guiding him to his feet. In the dim glow of the candles, I can see that he has tattoos all over his back and shoulders, but I can't make out what any of them are. My fingers trace along the inked skin. He's not overly muscular, but the muscles he does have are solid. Trailing my fingers down, I can feel his hard abs.

Holy bananas. There's eight of them.

Grabbing him by the hand, I lead him over to the bed. Gently, he lays me down and pulls my panties off. Getting comfortable next to me, he moves his hand between my legs. My pussy pulses, begging to be touched.

His fingertips lightly trace the outline of my lips. I wiggle and writhe on the bed, trying to encourage his fingers to touch where I desperately need them.

"Do you want me to rub your pretty pussy?" he asks.

I quickly nod and give a needy moan.

"Tell me what you want."

"Touch me," I plead.

"Where?"

I've never done much of the dirty talk thing. Judd was never into it, so I never even tried. But Tanner has barely even scratched the surface, and it's already turning me on like crazy.

Maybe it's the tequila. Maybe it's that I haven't been laid in forever. Or maybe it's that Tanner is hot as sin. Whatever it is, just about every single doubt I had is quickly fading away. I'm ready to go all the way.

Heck, I'm lying with my jiggly bits on full display, and I don't even care.

Decided to keep rolling with it, I say, "I want you to rub my clit."

He does as I ask and applies the perfect amount of pressure. "Tell me how you want it."

"Just like that," I moan. "Don't move."

My eyes roll back in my head as I get lost in how good it feels.

Not wanting to keep the pleasure all to myself, I reach down with one hand and clumsily unbutton his jeans. It takes a minute, but I manage to yank them down enough to pull out his dick.

Feeling it through his jeans didn't do it justice. The thing feels massive in my hands.

As I start to stroke it, he lets out a low growl.

"You're making it hard to focus here, beautiful," he says.

"Good."

He returns the favor, though, when he sucks my nipple into his mouth. My core starts to tighten as I get closer to my orgasm.

"Faster," I beg, and he increases his speed. Pleasure washes over me like a tidal wave. My entire body quakes as my moans fill the air.

"Yeah, Erin, let me hear it."

My mind goes completely blank as I come undone. Tanner continues to lightly rub me through the orgasm, which seems to last forever.

When I open my eyes again, I see him bringing his fingers to his mouth to lick off my juices.

"So sweet," he says. "Later on, I'm going to eat this pussy. But right now, I need to fuck you."

No complaints here.

He quickly stands up and pulls a condom out of his wallet. My eyes stay fixed on him as he removes his pants the rest of the way and rolls on the rubber. I don't need a lot of light to see how big and impressive he is.

He climbs on top of me, leaning down to kiss me while he slowly slides inside. In an instant, I remember how good sex can feel and how much I've missed it. Tanner fills me entirely, pushing in and out, every move deliberate. His lips move from mine to trail kisses along my neck and chest and then back again. My nails run down his back as my ankles lock around him.

Something about this one-night stand feels like *more* than a one-night-stand. There seems to be some sort of connection between us right now. But I tell myself that I'm just being insane.

I try to just enjoy he and I being locked in this passionate little bubble and enjoy the ride. And maybe it's time I take a ride of my own.

I gently push Tanner off me and move on top of him. I try not to think about my not-so-perky boobs or my chubby stomach. Instead, I decide to live in the moment.

Because after tonight, I'll never see this guy again.

Right?

Chapter Six

TANNER

Holy shit, this woman is sexy. I want to fuck her all night long, but I'm not sure how long I'll last with the way she's riding me.

When we first started, I could tell she was feeling self-conscious. That was clear when she kept the lights off. But I don't mind fucking her by candlelight. She still looks beautiful. And she has absolutely nothing to be self-conscious about.

Because damn.

I love a woman with curves. I want to kiss, lick, and worship every inch of her.

My hands roam all over her skin as she slowly moves up and down. Her pussy squeezes me as she slides all the way up to the head of my cock. I want to pull her down and kiss her, but I'm enjoying the view way too much.

Her hair falls behind her as she throws her head back. Her eyes close as she softly moans, and her skin glows in the soft candlelight.

Her hands brace on my chest, giving her the leverage she needs. And also pushing her giant tits together. I make a mental note to slide my dick in between them later.

My hands move up to play with her nipples. Every time I pinch them, I feel her pussy tighten around me even more.

My only regret about this evening is that I took out my Prince Albert piercing yesterday and haven't put it back in yet. I've learned that women love it. Hopefully, I'll get another chance to fuck Erin with it in.

And hopefully, she lets me spend more time with her in general. I'd like to get to know her better—with and without her clothes on. I'd especially love to know why someone hasn't scooped her up yet. I'm not complaining, but it's surprising.

I didn't expect the night to end this way. Did I want it to?

Fuck yeah.

But I would've settled for a kiss or even just her phone number.

Now that we are here, though, I consider myself one lucky son-of-a-bitch. And I plan on enjoying every second.

Part of that means making her come again. There's no way I'm only giving her one orgasm.

"Turn around, beautiful," I tell her. "Let me see that perfect ass."

She looks a little confused but turns around anyway. I position her so that she's sitting reverse-cowgirl. She slowly sinks onto me, and I grit my teeth, trying not to immediately blow my load.

I grab ahold of her hips, grinding them against me harder and faster. Her hands cover mine as she rides me like she's in a damn rodeo.

But I'm guessing she's not going to get off on fucking alone. She's going to need more.

"Lean forward," I tell her. Gently, I push her forward enough until her palms hit the mattress.

I grab a pillow and prop it behind my head. My cock slides out of her, and I have the most perfect view of her sweet pink pussy. I slide two fingers into her wet opening and angle them toward her g-spot.

"Oh, fuck, Tanner," she moans.

I take my other hand and use my thumb to rub her clit. She pushes back against me, signaling just how much she loves it. Almost immediately, I can feel her pussy squeezing my fingers.

She still moans all kinds of curse words, but they're becoming more and more incoherent as she succumbs to the pleasure.

I can't tell she's getting close. To send her over the edge, I massage her clit, squeezing it between my thumb and finger.

"Tanner!" She screams as she starts to come. My eyes stay glued to her the entire time. Her ass jiggles as she struggles to sit still, and her pussy pulses.

It may be the sexiest thing I've ever seen.

When she's too sensitive for me to keep going, I move my hands away.

Slightly out of breath, she says, "Whoa. That was… wow."

"We aren't done yet, beautiful."

I move out from underneath her but keep her on her hands and knees. When she sees me line myself up behind her, she leans her chest forward and sticks her ass in the air.

"Damn girl. Look at this ass." I spend a moment rubbing her ass cheeks before slipping back inside.

I waste no time in increasing my pace. I pump in and out of her hard and fast. The way her ass shakes with every thrust, and the way her pussy milks my cock, I know this isn't going to last long. My balls ache, anxious for me to give her my release.

Erin moans my name, and it sounds so fucking hot coming from her lips.

When she begins moving her hips in tandem with me so that I fuck into her harder, I'm done. My balls tighten as I fill the condom. I let out a loud moan of my own before we fall into a tired heap.

"That was incredible," she says as her chest heaves.

"Fuck yes, it was," I agree. "Want to go for round two?"

She looks at me and giggles. "Let me catch my breath first."

I quickly get up to throw the condom away before joining her back in bed.

When I lay back down next to her, I'm surprised when she immediately cuddles up to me. My cock already is eager to dive back in for more, but with Erin's head on my chest, it takes mere moments before we are both asleep.

Chapter Seven

ERIN

My eyes slowly open, letting in the sunlight that peeks through the window. I make yet another mental note to get blackout curtains.

My body stretches while my tongue licks the top of my mouth.

What the heck is that horrible taste?

Tequila.

Everything from last night comes flooding back.

I sang karaoke.

I played pool.

I brought a guy home.

And he spent the night!

I really didn't intend for that part to happen. I figured we'd have some fun, and then Tanner would escape into the night. But when he fucked me into a literal after-sex coma, I couldn't keep my eyes open any longer.

I won't even go into the fact that sleeping next to someone again felt nice because I'm positive that is just the tequila talking.

My eyes go wide as I quickly feel the bed next to me.

No Tanner.

Did he finally come to his senses? Did he see my jiggly thirty-three-year-old body in the harsh light of day and head for the hills?

I practically jump out of my skin when I hear the toilet flush.

He's still here.

Not having the confidence that the tequila provided last night, I pull the sheet up around me, trying to cover up everything from the neck down.

I hear the water run, and I'm thankful I managed to pick a guy who washes his hands. I brace myself for him to open the door. What if he isn't as attractive as he was last night? What if the bad decision juice just provided a smoke screen of hotness?

But as he opens the door, I realize there's no smoke screen.

Only a smoke show.

He's somehow hotter than he was last night—if that's even possible.

And holy Toledo, he's still naked. I try not stare at the giant piece of man meat swinging between his legs, but it's hard.

Well, *it's* not hard.

It's just hanging there.

It has no business being that big without even being aroused.

Look at his face. Look at his face.

When my eyes finally travel up to the safe zone, I see that smile. Maybe it's not so safe.

You know how they say Helen of Troy was the face that launched a thousand ships? Tanner's smile could drop a thousand panties.

"Good morning, beautiful," he says.

I try to tell myself that now's about the time I should ask him to leave and get back to reality, but something inside me just can't.

"Morning," I reply with a smile. "How'd you sleep?"

What a dumb question to ask.

"Pretty damn good." He starts walking toward me. "But I planned on making you come a whole lot more before the exhaustion set in."

Just hearing him talk about making me come gets my body all tingly.

He slides back into bed next to me, but I don't move the sheet from around me just yet.

He asks, "What are your plans today, beautiful?"

Tell him your busy. Tell him you have work... church... to feed your llama. Anything. You don't need to keep this little fantasy of yours going on any longer.

But as though his big, swinging penis has some sort of mysterious hold on me, I instead say, "I don't think I have any plans. What about you?"

He puts his hand on my shoulder and lightly trails his fingertips across my skin. "Well, feel free to say no to this, but I was thinking you and I could spend some more time together... naked. And in the process, get to know each other a little better."

I tuck a rogue strand of hair behind my ear. "I'm not going to lie. That sounds great, but I need to ask you something first."

"Ask away."

"Why me?"

His forehead creases. "What do you mean?"

"I mean, why did you hit on *me*? I'm clearly older than you and at least fifty pounds overweight. I'm sure you could have had any pick of girls in the bar. The ones who were drooling over you when you were singing seemed more your type."

He thinks for a mere moment before saying, "Yeah, they were cute. But so are you—gorgeous in fact—and you actually have something interesting to say."

"I guess," I mutter under my breath.

I suddenly realize that while I was talking, the sheet that was wrapped around me has fallen down. Very self-conscious, I quickly yank it back into position.

"Alright, we just can't have this," Tanner says sternly.

Has he finally come to his senses?

"Huh?" I ask, bracing myself for his answer.

"We can't have you thinking that those girls are any better than you. We can't have you thinking that you aren't absolutely fucking stunning." He speaks as he pulls down the sheet, exposing my bare breasts.

He starts kissing along my skin as he tells me what he thinks of how I look. I could make comments about how I think he should get his eyes checked, but I'm enjoying myself way too much. It's so refreshing to hear a man tell me how *good* he thinks I look instead of how I've let myself go.

Tanner stops kissing and looks at me. "How about we spend some more time together, and I show you how sexy I think you are?"

I know I should probably cut this off now and ask him to leave, but there's something keeping me from doing that.

"Okay," I reply with a smile.

Immediately, his lips find mine, and we start to kiss. He scoots next to me, moving the sheets, so our bodies press against each other. It doesn't take long for me to feel his Thunder Down Under pushing into my leg.

Just when we start to get hot and heavy, my phone chimes from the nightstand table.

"Hold that thought," I whisper to Tanner. "That's my doorbell camera."

I open up the app and am shocked to see Judd standing there.

What the--?

The microphone is broken, so I will have to go downstairs to see what he wants.

"I'll be back," I say, flying out of bed.

I quickly grab a t-shirt and a pair of shorts out of my drawer and head out of the room.

I open the door to Judd immediately snapping. "What the hell took you so long? Were you still in bed?"

"No, I—" I stop myself, not wanting to get into a fight with a naked man in my bed. "What do you want?"

"Chris forgot his football cleats. He has practice."

"Oh, one second." I shut the door to keep him from coming inside and quickly dig through the pile of shoes in the bottom of the closet. I find the grass-covered cleats and head toward the door.

When I hand them to Judd, he takes them and turns to leave. Before he steps off the porch, he says, "Just for once, Erin, I wish you'd get your shit together as a mother, so I don't have to come back here all the damn time."

When I shut the door once again, I stand still for a moment, trying to collect myself. I hear movement upstairs, and I remember Tanner is waiting on me. Suddenly, the reality of this whole situation punches me straight in the gut.

I'm a mom. And here I am playing grab-ass with some sexy guy I met in a bar.

What the hell am I doing?

Judd showing up is an excellent reminder of why I don't do things like this. It's why I spend any free time I have home alone. As great as this little break from reality has been, it's not my life.

I slowly make my way back upstairs, fully prepared to put an end to this whole thing.

When I walk inside, Tanner immediately notices that my demeanor has changed. "Hey, beautiful, you okay?"

"Yeah. Just a delivery," I lie. "Look, maybe this whole thing isn't a great idea?"

Confusion clouds his features. He stands up and walks over to me. "Hey, what happened? Five minutes ago, we were talking about spending more time together."

"Okay, before this conversation goes any further, I'm going to need you to put on some underwear at least. I can't have a serious conversation with your anaconda staring at me."

He laughs but still grabs his boxers and slides them on. Even with the layer of cotton blocking my view, I know what's underneath, and it's still distracting.

"Alright," he says. "Now, do you want to tell me what's changed in the past few minutes?"

I let out an obnoxiously loud sigh. "Tanner, you don't want to get involved with me. Heck, you don't want anything to do with me at all. You should run for the hills right now."

"Oh, yeah? Why's that?"

Gathering all my courage, I decide to come clean. "Look, Tanner, I know this may come as a surprise to you, but... I'm a mom."

I wait for his jaw to drop, or his eyes to pop out of his head in sheer surprise like a cartoon character. But his face remains exactly the same.

"Yeah, I kind of figured you had a kid." He says it like it's no big deal.

"How?" I ask. "There's no pictures anywhere around. Do I just give off some sort of mom aura or something?"

"Erin, you have Spiderman toys in your bathtub."

"Oh. Right."

Duh, Erin.

"I don't care that you have a kid. Doesn't bother me at all."

"Well, I don't just have *a* kid. I have three. Three boys."

"Is that supposed to scare me off? I like kids. Besides, I'm not asking you for some big commitment here. I'm just asking you to let us get to know each other better and see what happens."

"I'm telling you that you don't want to get to know me."

He takes a seat on the edge of the bed. "Why do you say that?"

Oh, boy. This is going to be a whole can of worms that he's going to wish he hadn't opened.

"Because I'm a mess. A thirty-three-year-old mess. That's right. I'm a whopping eight years older than you. I'm no spring chicken, and I've got the body to prove it."

He interrupts me to say, "I love your body."

"Well, last night, in the dark, you couldn't see my cellulite. Or my stretchmarks. Or the C-section scar from my third kid. In fact, everything from last night was all smoke and mirrors. My outfit? I don't dress like that. My wardrobe consists of leggings and old t-shirts—most of which have been thrown up on by my kids at some point. And my sexy bra and panties? Those live in the bottom of my drawer, barely seeing the light of day. Most of my undergarments don't look like that. Most days, I wear no makeup, big glasses, and a messy bun. Tanner, I have only been with three guys my entire life. And up until last night, I had been with the same one for over thirteen years. And even though he and I are divorced, he still makes my life miserable. When I'm not working my nine-to-five job, I'm taking kids to practice or doing laundry. I have zero time for any semblance of a social life. Every other weekend my kids go to their dad's, and it's the one time that I get to do anything for myself. Usually, I stay home and drink wine and read romance books, but last night, my friends convinced me to go out. My point is that I don't have time for any type of relationship."

When I come up for air, I look at Tanner in all of his tattooed glory. He has this half-grin on his face that I can't quite get a read on.

"Say something," I prompt.

"Did you say your kids are gone all weekend?"

"What? Yes," I stammer. "What does that have to do with anything?"

"When was the last time someone took care of you? The last time someone made you feel beautiful and sexy? When was the last time a man made your toes curl?"

"Last night," I answer, not having to think about it.

"I mean before that."

Okay, that question's a little harder.

When I take a while to answer, Tanner says, "That's what I thought."

He holds out his hands for mine. I take it, and he pulls me toward him. "Maybe it's about time someone made you feel good for once."

"Oh? And you want to be that person?"

"Fuck yes, I do." He wraps his arms around my waist and looks up at me. "As for your body, I know what it looks like. We were in candlelight, but I'm not blind. I love the way your body looks, and I want to worship every inch of it."

I suck it my breath as he raises my t-shirt, exposing my less-than-flattering stomach.

"I don't care about stretchmarks," he says, planting a few kisses on my body.

"Or your C-section scar."

Another kiss.

An unexpected wave of tears stings my eyes. I was married for over ten years, and my husband never made me feel as good as this man that I've basically known for ten minutes.

I still can't believe it's all happening.

Running my fingers through his hair, I still think he's crazy. But this smoke show of a man is telling me he wants to spend the weekend calling me pretty and giving me orgasms.

Who am I to say no to that?

"Okay, Fabio," I say. "Show me what you've got."

Chapter Eight

ERIN

"First of all," Tanner begins. "Let's take these clothes back off. Oh, and for the record, I don't care what clothes or panties you have on because I know what's underneath."

"Anyone ever told you you're smoother than butter?" I tease.

"Maybe," he says with a wink.

Lord, that wink is going to get me in trouble.

Maybe I should have asked him to leave, but the thought of him being here actually makes me excited. And I can't remember the last time I was excited about anything. For once, I'm going to do something for me without worrying about everyone else in the world.

He grabs the bottom of my t-shirt and slowly pulls it over my head. The natural sunlight coming through the windows shows absolutely everything. There's no hiding in shadows or candlelight now.

But Tanner's eyes still move all over my body like he thinks I'm gorgeous. I haven't felt anything like this in so long.

His large hands start on my thighs and slowly rub upward until they get to my hips. His fingers sink in as he grabs a handful.

"Damn, woman" he growls. "These hips are going to make me fall in love with you."

He pulls me toward him until I find myself straddling him.

He runs his hand through my messy hair, pushing it out of my face so that he has a clear path to my lips. Those crystal blue eyes of his look into mine as he slowly pulls me toward him. I swear I could look into those eyes all day. They're hypnotizing. He could convince me to do anything, and I'd do it without question.

He kisses me, grabbing my lips with his before his tongue flicks against mine. It doesn't take long for the kiss to turn passionate.

Pulling back, he says, "You ready to see what my pierced tongue can do?"

The mere thought of his skillful tongue between my legs makes my lady bits flutter with excitement.

Before I can answer his question, he lifts me with my legs around him and tosses me in the middle of the soft mattress. As he gets situated between my legs, I can already see the tent he's pitching in his boxers. The fact that I can do that to him makes me feel so sexy.

Laying on his stomach, he pushes my thighs apart so that I'm completely on display. Self-doubt hits me for a moment. I mean, I've pushed a few humans out of there. It's not exactly perfect.

But it doesn't seem to matter to Tanner. He takes one finger and runs it down the length of my slit.

"Such a pretty pussy," he whispers. His breath hitting the sensitive flesh sends shivers down my spine.

I close my eyes and get ready to try to enjoy the moment. It's always felt good to have my pussy eaten, but I've never been able to come this way. Probably because Judd never stayed down there long enough to get the job done. My mind gets in the way too much. Do I smell? Does it taste bad? Why's it taking so long? Does his jaw hurt?

Makes it hard to concentrate.

I enjoy a guy going down on me for what I know it is—a precursor to sex. But it still feels good.

I feel Tanner use his thumbs to spread me open. Next thing I know, I feel his tongue against my clit. I let out a soft moan at the contact. His tongue ring touches the tiny pearl as he pulls back the hood.

My quiet moans turn into a full-blown scream as my whole body bucks off the bed.

I'm not sure if it's the tongue ring or his attention to that sensitive area, but holy crap. It feels incredible. His licks are light and slow so as to not make it too much to handle. He waits until I get used to it before increasing his tempo or pressure.

My eyes squeeze shut as my hands cover my face. It's not that I'm embarrassed. I'm just not quite sure what else to do with them.

But Tanner seems to have some thoughts.

"Hey, beautiful. Look at me," he commands.

Slowly, I open my eyes to gaze down at him. His blue eyes stare up at me while his tongue gives me a long lick.

He says, "I want you to watch while I make this pussy come with my mouth. Tell me what you like."

"All of it," I moan. "Just don't stop."

His tongue gets back to work, driving me insane. It alternates between licking circles around my clit to flicking against it. My thighs begin to tremble as the pleasure inside me slowly builds.

And I mean *slowly.* This is not a sprint. It's a freaking marathon. Poor Tanner is probably going to have lockjaw by the time it's all said and done.

I feel bad that it's taking forever, and it's messing with my head. Apparently, I'm making it pretty obvious that my mind is taking over.

Tanner stops and moves from between my legs. He crawls up my body until we're face to face.

I figure he's had enough of trying to get me off and is ready to jump into the main event.

"Erin, what's wrong?" He asks.

"What do you mean?"

"I mean, you seemed to really be enjoying yourself, but then, you totally shut down. Did I do something wrong? Did something not feel good?"

"No!" I exclaim. "Everything feels amazing. It's just..."

"Talk to me," he begs.

"I feel like it takes forever for me to come, and I know it's probably not enjoyable for you. I feel bad.

And to be honest, I'm not even sure it's possible for me to get off like that."

"Why do you think that?"

"No one has ever stayed down there long enough to find out."

"Okay, listen here, beautiful. I love eating pussy. In fact, it's one of my essential food groups. Why do you think I have a tongue ring? And I don't give a shit how long it takes. I'll stay down here all damn day."

"But your mouth will hurt."

"I promise I'll be fine." He leans down and lightly kisses my lips. "I want you to try to clear that big, beautiful mind of yours and just let it feel good."

"What if I can't come?"

"Oh, I think you can. And I intend to do my best to make it happen. I love a good challenge."

He moves back down and gets to work once more. And this time, he's a man on a mission. His tongue zeroes in on that perfect little sweet spot and makes it feel incredible.

My trembling legs struggle to sit still as I find myself finally letting go and getting lost in the moment. And much to my surprise, I feel myself climbing toward an orgasm.

Tanner sucks my swollen clit into his mouth and runs his tongue ring against it. That makes me start squirming in every direction, but he hooks his arms around my legs to hold me in place. Not knowing what to do with myself, I fist my hands in Tanner's hair and hang on for dear life as the orgasm takes hold. The moment it begins, I can barely sit still, but he holds me still and keeps licking through the entire thing.

When I'm too sensitive to take anymore, he gives my clit one final kiss before whispering, "Good girl. I knew this pussy could come with my tongue."

I've never been called a good girl, but I like it.

A lot.

Tanner stands up to grab a condom out of his wallet, and I wonder just how many of those he has in there. I sit up and grab him by the hand, yanking him hard enough that he falls onto the bed.

He grins at me as I take the rubber out of his hand and tear the corner with my teeth. As I pull it out of the wrapper, I try to remember the last time, before last night, that I actually used one of these. High school?

Well, that thought makes me feel old.

I examine it for a moment to make sure I'm putting it on the right way.

"Take your boxers off, Fabio," I tell him.

He quickly shimmies out of them, so I can have easier access. Before I roll the condom on, something catches my eye.

There's a hole in his dick.

Well, I mean, aside from the normal hole.

There's TWO holes in his dick.

"Uhm, Tanner. What happened?" I ask, a little nervous to know the answer.

His eyes flick down to see what I'm talking about. A wicked little smile plays on his lips.

"Nothing happened, beautiful. I've got my dick pierced."

"Come again?" There's no way I heard him correctly.

"My cock is pierced with a Prince Albert. I just don't have the ring in right now."

"Who's Albert?"

"That's just what it's called?"

"Didn't that hurt?"

He laughs. "Well, yes. It's my dick. It's pretty sensitive."

Confused as heck, I ask, "So, why do it?"

"Well, I originally did it as a dare, but I discovered something after I had done it."

"What?" I whisper as though someone else may be listening.

"It makes everyone involved in the sex feel *really* good. You ever been fucked by a pierced cock?"

"I think my overall reaction to this shows that the answer is no."

"Well, we will just have to change that once I put it back in."

Something about that intrigues me. Curiosity makes me want to find out how good it feels. But look how curiosity turned out for the cat.

I look down and realize that I still held the condom between my fingers. I figure this side trip has probably made him lost interest, but when I look, I see that his member is still standing at attention.

Man, it's big.

And thick.

And slightly curved.

This man could be a dildo model.

I start the condom at the tip and slowly roll it down, watching the rubber stretch around its girth.

"How do you want it, beautiful?" He asks.

"Any way you want to give it," I reply.

In one swift movement, he climbs on top of me and moves my ankles onto his shoulders. He pushes the big head of his dick inside me. I'm still so wet that he slides in easily.

As I look up at this gorgeous man who is pounding me seven ways to Sunday, I can't help but realize how surreal this whole thing seems.

In this moment, I'm not just a mom. I'm a woman—and a sexy one at that. Something like thirty-six hours from now, I'll be back to thinking about math homework and bake sales.

So, I figure I'd better enjoy this to the absolute fullest.

Chapter Nine

TANNER

With her chest heaving, Erin says, "Okay, if you are going to keep screwing my brains out, I'm going to need some food."

"Same. And we are going to need more condoms."

She looks at me and smiles. "You mean to tell me that you don't have a never-ending supply in that wallet of yours?"

"Surprisingly, no. I will do a Postmates order for some."

"A man who takes action. I like it." She lets out the cutest little giggle. "Want to go downstairs while I make us something to eat?"

"Of course."

I watch her get up and put on a t-shirt. My eyes stay glued to her ass until the cotton material covers it up. Then, I look away to find my boxers and slip them on.

Grabbing her for a quick kiss, I say, "Don't get used to that shirt. You won't be wearing it for long."

She smiles at me. "Good. I hate this shirt."

Before she walks out of the room, she turns back toward me. Her finger taps her lips as she thinks.

"Before we go any further, I need to ask you something."

I brace myself for what she might say.

"I probably should have asked this last night before we got all sweaty and naked, but tequila makes me forget things. What is your last name?"

She's adorable.

"Samson," I tell her. "How about you?"

"Prescott." She grins. "Okay, now we can go eat."

Five minutes later, I'm watching Erin dig through her pantry and fridge. I like when she bends over, and I catch a glimpse of her pussy peeking between her legs.

Frazzled, she says, "Okay, I don't have a ton to work with here. Most everything I have is something that's on the list of my kids' favorites. How do you feel about dino nuggets and mac and cheese?"

"Sounds just fine to me."

"Are you sure?" She looks worried. "I just didn't get the chance to grocery shop this week."

"Erin, it's not a big deal," I tell her. "Normally, I'm living out of a take-out sack, so anything you want to cook sounds just fine with me."

"Wow," she says, looking more than a little surprised.

"What?" I ask.

"Nothing. It's just that if I ever tried to feed my ex-husband dino nuggets and mac and cheese, I never would have heard the end of it. He would have thrown it in the trash right in front of me."

I'm tempted to ask who the fuck she was married to, but I don't want to overstep any boundaries.

So, I just say, "Believe me when I say that if you are willing to take the time to make me something to eat, I'm not going to be ungrateful enough to complain."

She gives me a smile and asks if I want something to drink.

"Sure."

She opens the fridge and stares inside for a moment before handing me a bottle of water. "Man, I really need to go grocery shopping. Pretty soon, the kids will start rioting."

"Eh, I'm sure running around after three kids occupies most of your time."

"You have no idea. They're a handful." She quickly realizes what she said could be taken the wrong way and adds, "Not that I'm complaining. I mean, I love being a mom."

"I have no doubt that you are great mom."

"What makes you say that?" She asks. "You don't really know me."

She's right. I don't. But as I slowly start to learn more, I'm liking all of it.

"True. But the fact that you worry about if you're a good mom means that you probably are."

She gives me a small smile. "I guess so." As she arranges the dino nuggets on a cookie sheet, she changes the subject. "So, you said you have a job where you travel a lot?"

"Yeah, I do flooring for commercial buildings. Mostly supermarkets and things like that. I'm usually gone for a week or two at a time."

"Have you gone anywhere cool?"

My shoulders shrug. "Depends on what you consider cool. Mostly, my work is all around Texas, Arkansas, and Arizona. I've been to California a couple of times. The beach was nice, but I was working too much to enjoy it."

She gets some water boiling for the macaroni. "Traveling that much has got to be hard."

"Eh, it can be. It used to really fuck with my sleep, but over the years, I've adapted. Now, I can start catching z's pretty much anywhere."

Her nose crinkles as she gives me a cute smile. "Oh, yeah. With three kids, I've mastered that particular skill."

Looking at this woman, I still find it hard to believe that she's a mother of three. Erin may be eight years older than me, but she doesn't look like it. She's drop-dead gorgeous. It's obvious that her ex-husband has destroyed her self-esteem—which pisses me off because this woman deserves to be shown every damn day how sexy she is.

I know she said that she isn't looking for any type of relationship, so at this point, I will take what I can get. If that means just spending a weekend trying to convince her that she's beautiful, that's fine with me.

"Yeah," I say. "I imagine that with three kids, you've had a lot of sleepless nights."

"When they were babies, it was the worst. Now the sleepless nights only really come when they're sick. Or when I'm kept up by my own anxiety." Immediately, after she stops talking, she once again looks embarrassed that she was talking about her kids.

Not wanting her to feel that way, I say, "Why don't you tell me about your kids?"

Her cheeks blush a little. "You don't want to hear about that."

"Why wouldn't I?"

"Because hearing about me being a mom isn't all that interesting."

"Erin, let me tell you something," I begin. "I've hung out with a whole lot of women—many of them my age or younger. A good number of them couldn't see past where they were going to go dancing on Friday nights. While that's all well and good, I enjoy finding someone who has more to say. With three kids, you've probably had a good amount of actual life experience."

She stops me to say, "Tanner, there's a big difference between having some life experience and really getting out there and living. I'm sure you have me beat in that department."

I walk over to her and tuck a strand of hair behind her ear. "Well, then, little lady, I think we could learn a thing or two from one another."

"Oh, yeah?" The corners of her lips twitch as though she's trying not to smile.

"Yep. Because my problem seems to be that I do too much living. Sometimes, I really suck at having my shit together."

Erin throws her head back and lets out a loud cackle. "Oh, honey, life experience does not mean that I have my shit together...like at all."

I smile. "Something else we have in common."

She goes to grab a spatula off one end of the counter and knocks over a half-full glass of water. The liquid quickly flows toward me and gets my phone wet.

"Oh, crap!" She squeals. As quickly as she can, she grabs a dish towel out of the drawer and picks up my phone to wipe it off. "I'm so sorry. I'm so clumsy."

By the way she's apologizing, I get the feeling that something like this would have made her ex more than a little upset. Wanting to try to help her, I reach for some paper towels and wipe the remaining water up before it gets to some of the papers on the edge of the counter.

She hands my phone back to me and says she's sorry once again. Without even taking the time to look at it, I set it on the counter and grab her by the hand.

Pulling her toward me, I say, "Hey, it's alright. Just a little bit of water."

"What if I ruined your phone?" She asks with wide, worried eyes.

"Then, I get a new phone. It's not the end of the world."

She looks like she doesn't believe me, so I lean down to give her a kiss just to drive the point home. Maybe it actually worked because when I pull back, she smiles at me.

As she adds the macaroni to the water, I see a frame on one end of the counter and walk over to grab it. There are three little boys, all with Erin's dark hair.

"Are these your kids?" I ask.

Without missing a beat, she says, "Nope. Just the insert that came in the frame."

I laugh. "Sarcasm. I like it." Looking down at the photo again, I add, "Good looking kids."

"Yeah, they drive me nuts, but I wouldn't trade them for anything."

"I think most mommas would share the same sentiment. How old are they?"

She stirs the macaroni. "Chris is thirteen. Alex is eight. And Joey is three, almost four."

"Are they all in school?"

"Alex and Chris are, but Joey is just in daycare. Thankfully, he will start Kindergarten next year. Daycare is expensive as heck."

"Man, I can barely take care of myself, let alone three other human beings."

She shrugs her shoulders. "Eh, I've been doing it for so long now that it's just life. I wouldn't know anything different."

"Fair enough."

A few minutes later, she's plated us up some food, and we are sitting on her couch.

"What do you do for work?" I ask her. I feel like maybe I'm bombarding her with questions, but I'm just trying to learn as much as I can in the short amount of time that we have.

"I'm a receptionist at a dentist office."

"Do you get free dental work?" I ask.

She laughs. "Yeah. But seeing all the horror stories that I do, I'm super meticulous about how I take care of my teeth."

"I am too, but I eat so much candy I'm pretty sure the two things cancel each other out."

"What's your favorite candy?" She asks between bites.

"Oh, hell, I don't know. I'll eat any of it. Any sour gummies are a safe bet, though. What about you?"

"I'm not a big sweets person."

Acting shocked, I pretend like I'm going to get up and leave. "Well, this has been fun, but I don't think this is going to work."

She giggles so hard she snorts.

Holy fuck, that's adorable.

"If you're not a *sweets* person, what exactly do you eat when you have a craving? Please don't say something like kale. I don't know that I could take it."

"Follow me. I'll show you."

I stand up and go with her into the kitchen. She opens up the door to her refrigerator and points to the door.

"Whoa," I say, shocked by the sheer number of pickle jars. Every kind of pickles you can imagine.

"Yeah." She nods. Opening up one of the cabinets, she shows that she has a whole other stash in there. "I have a bit of a problem."

"Do you really like pickles that much?"

"Yep. My whole life…except when I was pregnant. Then, I couldn't stand them."

"You're just an interesting little bird, aren't you?"

She laughs. "The pickle thing might be the most interesting thing about me."

I doubt that.

We go back to the couch to finish eating all while getting to know each other better. When we finish, she says, "Tell me something about you that not a lot of people know."

"You mean besides that I'm a serial killer?" I joke.

She gives me a monotone "ha ha".

I think for a moment before answering. "I'm a huge nerd."

"What. No way."

"I'm completely serious."

Doubt is written all over her face. "Can you elaborate?"

"I love all of the crazy fantasy movies and the books they're based off of. Love playing World of Warcraft. All of it. Harry Potter is one of my favorite things in the world."

"I've never actually sat down and watched the movies."

"What?" I cry. "How?"

"I mean, I've seen bits and pieces, and I think I read the first book when I was a kid."

"Oh, we are going to have to fix that," I tell her. "How about Lord of the Rings?"

"Haven't seen those either."

"Game of Thrones?"

"Nope."

My mouth hangs open, and Erin laughs. "Better shut that thing before a bug flies in. I'm sorry, but how can you look like that and also be a nerd?"

"What is it that you think I look like?" I ask with a teasing smile.

She rolls her eyes. "Don't do that. You know that you are practically sex on a stick. Aren't nerds not generally great with women?"

"I don't think the two are mutually exclusive." I laugh. "I can like nerdy things and still know how to make a woman come. How is it that you haven't seen any of this good stuff?"

She shrugs her shoulders. "Normally, when I have my kids, we are always watching either cartoons or superhero movies. I've definitely seen all of those."

"And when you don't have your kids?"

"I don't watch a lot, but I read a whole lot of romance novels—the dirty kind."

"How dirty?"

Her eyes look into mine. "Dirty. I think it's my own little escape into another world. One that's more exciting than mine. I get to read about all the sexy stuff I want to try but have never gotten to."

"We're not all that different. I watch the nerdy movies for the same reasons. It's a nice escape."

She smiles. "Yeah, I get that."

"But you know the one big difference between my movies and your books?"

"What's that?"

"I'm never going to go to Hogwarts or Mordor, but we sure as shit can act out some of the scenes from those books of yours."

Chapter Ten

ERIN

"You want to act out scenes from my books?" I ask, a little in disbelief.

Tanner sets his hand on my thigh as he scoots closer to me. "Do you read those books and think about all those dirty things being done to you?"

"Maybe," I reply, trying to be coy.

His hands push my knees apart, exposing my lady bits to him. Normally, I'd be worried that I'm gross from not showering yet, but right now, all I can focus on is Tanner looking at me.

"Erin," he begins. "Do you read those books and then play with this pretty pussy thinking about it?"

His thumb gives light, feathery touches to my sensitive lips, and my breath hitches in my throat. "Sometimes."

More like every time I read a sexy scene when my kids aren't home.

When I was married, I never dabbled much in the world of *self-exploration.* One, Judd didn't approve. He was of the mindset that a husband should be the only one giving his wife pleasure.

And two, ninety-nine percent of the time, I was far too exhausted to be turned on in any way whatsoever. Most days I barely had enough energy to make it from the couch to the bed, let alone double click my mouse once I get there.

When I got divorced, I suddenly had a lot more free time and a huge need to release some tension. It was then that I discovered the wonderful world of vibrators.

And I do mean *wonderful.*

Tanner continues to tease, not touching me quite where I want him to. "Tell me how you make yourself come."

Not knowing how he will respond, I whisper, "With my vibrator."

In one fluid motion, he pulls me into his lap so that I'm straddling him. "That is so fucking sexy," he groans before pressing his lips to mine.

Our kiss is hot and frenzied—all fire and passion. I can't remember the last time I enjoyed making out this much. I can't seem to get enough.

I feel Tanner's hard length poking me through his boxers. Grinding against it, I get a guttural reaction from him. His fingertips grip into my ass, pushing me even further onto him.

With a fierce growl, he breaks the kiss and curses. "Fuck! We need more condoms."

My lip pokes out in a pout, but I know that he's right. He grabs his phone off the table and opens Postmates.

"Is your phone working okay?" I nervously ask.

"Just fine, beautiful," he replies with a smile.

I felt awful when I knocked water all over it earlier, but thankfully, he didn't make me feel any worse. Judd would have yelled at me for being so clumsy.

Night and day.

"Okay, condoms," he mumbles as he adds them to the cart. "Can you think of anything else we need?"

"Hmm." I think for a moment. "Well, we may need something else to eat since we finished off the dino nuggets."

He looks up at me. "How do you feel about fajitas and margaritas?"

Before I can say anything, he says, "Oh, crap. You had margaritas last night, didn't you? Probably don't want them again, huh?"

"For starters, I will never turn down margaritas," I tell him. "And I love fajitas. But you want to cook for me?"

"Of course. Why is that weird?"

"It's not," I reply, hesitant to tell him that I've never had a man cook for me that wasn't my father. The only thing Judd would ever do was grill some meat, and even then, the rest of the meal fell on my shoulders.

"So, fajitas sound good?"

"Sounds perfect," I tell him.

Tanner Samson seems to be full of surprises. At first glance, you'd never think that this tatted and pierced man secretly has a huge sweet spot.

He clicks a few more buttons on his phone before setting it back down on the coffee table. "Alright. Done. Should be here within an hour or so."

"Hmmm." I tap my finger on my chin. "What could we do for an hour?"

My hand slowly trails up his thigh, and he immediately understands what kind of game I'm playing.

As serious as a heart attack, he says, "Well, I could eat your pussy until the condoms come."

"As much as I would love that," I begin. "I think I need to go take a shower first."

"Want some company?"

"Sure." I smile, which gets him cheesing like a fool.

When he gets up from the couch, he holds out his hand for mine. I take it, and he pulls me in for a quick kiss before leading me upstairs to my bathroom.

When we get there, he looks from my oversized bathtub to me and back again. "Would you rather take a bath?"

"You want to take a bath?" I ask in disbelief.

"I get to look at you naked and covered in bubbles? Sign me up."

I love bubble baths, so I'm not about to turn that down. But I can't say that I've ever had company in the tub before.

This should be fun.

A few minutes later, I have the Spiderman toys removed, the water, filled, and the bubbles added. I step in and get comfortable while waiting for Tanner to join me. As he removes his boxers, I'm once again in awe of his dick.

He raises one leg over the side of the tub and starts to lower it into the water. The moment his toes hit the surface, he yanks his foot back.

"Holy fuck, that's hot!"

I start laughing hard enough to snort. "Do you want me to add some cold water?"

He takes a deep breath and puffs out his chest. "No. I will get used to it. Just make sure to clean up the mess if my skin melts off."

It takes a minute, but he manages to finally sit down. I try to stifle my giggles as I watch him sink into the hot water.

"You good?" I ask, barely managing to keep a straight face.

"Yep. How did you get in here all willy-nilly? You just stepped in like it was room temperature."

"I like it hot."

"Guess so," he says with a small chuckle.

Charlie comes wandering into the room, the tags on his collar jingling the entire way.

Tanner cocks his eyebrow at me. "Has this dog been here the whole time?"

"Yes. Tanner, meet Charlie. Charlie has severe anxiety, so he has his own space down in the mud room along with a doggie door to go in and out as he pleases. When he heard someone new here, he probably went into hiding."

Tanner holds his hand out for the dog to sniff. I expect the dog to shuffle out of the room as quickly as he came in. New people freak him out—especially men. He even wigged out when our Amazon driver tried to give him a dog biscuit.

I'm shocked when the dog sniffs his hand before giving it a couple licks. And then he actually lays down next to the tub.

"Holy cow," I say. "I think he actually likes you."

"Is that weird?" He asks, reaching down to pet Charlie's head.

"This dog doesn't like anyone besides us. He's scared of anyone and anything."

"Maybe Charlie is an excellent judge of character." He winks at me. "When did he lose his leg?"

"He got hit by a car right out front. My kids found him, and that's how we came to adopt him. Judging from how skittish he is, I'm guessing he was abused before that happened, though."

"Poor guy," he says with more pets to Charlie's head.

"Do you have any animals?"

"Nah. I'd love to, but I don't think it would be fair to an animal with as much as I travel. And unfortunately, most of the hotels I stay at aren't pet-friendly. Sometimes, I go steal my brother's dog, George, though, and take him to the park for a while."

"Fair enough. You could get a reptile or something. My oldest has a snake, and honestly, the snake is pretty low maintenance."

He holds up his hand to stop me. "Whoa. You have a snake? Is he here?" He whispers as though the snake might hear him.

"Mm-hmm. He's a milk snake and is really nice."

Jokingly, he goes to stand up. "Well, I'll see you around."

Grabbing him by the arm, I yank him back, making the water slosh everywhere. "Oh, sit down. He's in his tank. He's not going anywhere. Are you really that scared of a little snake?" I start making chicken noises at him.

"Snakes eat people, Erin," he says with all the conviction in the world.

"Tanner, there's no way this snake could eat you. Heck, the snake in your pants is probably bigger than him. You don't have to worry about Tater Tot."

"You named him Tater Tot?"

"My kids named him. Are you really going to be scared of something with a name like that?"

He nods. "Absolutely. Why would you buy a man-eating creature like a snake?"

"I'm not the one who bought it," I tell him. "My children's father thought it would be a great gift. Since Chris lives here, it made more sense to keep the snake here. Truth be told, I think he bought it because he thought it would freak me out. Out of all the battles I fight, having a snake wasn't the hill I was willing to die on."

He lets out an involuntary shiver as if just thinking about the snake gives him the heebie-jeebies. "I'll stick with Charlie here. He's much cuter than any ol' snake."

I take a handful of bubbles and put them on the side of the tub as the dog playfully starts biting at them.

I watch Tanner mimic my actions and play with the dog. How is it that twenty-four hours ago, I was at work, dreading going out with my friends because it meant I had to leave my romance novels and my sweatpants. Now, I'm sitting with a hot, tatted, and pierced man with a big dick in my bathtub. A man who tells me and *shows* me how sexy he thinks I am.

It's almost as though I'm living my own little romance novel.

The shock of it all is still overwhelming. After being with the same man for so long and being so unhappy, I never thought I'd open up so easily to another man. Yet somehow, Tanner makes me feel at ease enough to relax and just enjoy the moment. Sitting here with him makes me forget about all the baggage I carry around with me.

I figure it's because I know that this whole thing is temporary. After tomorrow, I'll go back to being a busy mom, and Tanner will go find another woman to give countless orgasms to.

I'm about to learn that my baggage can't be so easily forgotten about, though.

Tanner says, "Can I ask you something?"

"Sure. But I don't guarantee I'll answer," I reply with a small smile.

"Understood." He takes a deep breath before continuing. "Alright, I may not have known you all that long, but in the time that I've gotten to know you, I can see how awesome you are. You are funny, sexy as hell, and clearly a great mom. What kind of idiot of a man would give you up?"

I sit quietly for a moment, trying to figure out if I want to open up this can of worms.

It's a pretty big can.

I rarely ever talk to anyone about my divorce. Although the people close to me know the details, quite frankly, it's no one else's business. Not to mention the fact that I try not to shed any negative light on the father of my children. I encourage others to do the same as not to influence my kids to feel one way or another about their daddy.

Sometimes, that can be a hard cross to bear. It's difficult keeping everything inside. I figure that maybe Tanner wouldn't be a terrible person to tell since this whole thing is short-lived. I assume anything I tell him will stay within our own little bubble that we've created for this weekend.

When I've been quiet a little too long, Tanner says, "I'm sorry. You don't have to talk about if you don't want to."

"It's alright. I'm just not really used to talking about it, but I don't mind."

Tanner takes one of my feet in his hands and starts rubbing it as I try to figure out where to start.

"Judd and I have known each other forever. We both dated a couple other people before we got together in high school. He was the quarterback of the football team, and I was homecoming queen. It just made sense. And back then, he was sweeter than molasses. We had so much fun together. After we started having sex, he got a little more jealous than I would have liked, but I chalked it up to us both just being so young. We were going to go to college together, but I got in, and Judd didn't. He convinced me to put college on hold, so we could both work and save up money so that way he could move with me the next year. Looking back, it was so stupid. I never should have let a boy talk me into that because a year turned into three. Just when I was about to actually go back, I got pregnant."

I pause for a moment to take a breath. "I wasn't exactly thrilled about the idea of having a kid. It sounds terrible, but I had big plans, and I wasn't sure a baby would fit into any of them. Regardless, Judd and I ended up having a shotgun wedding in his parents' backyard. Judd became a cop and thought it would be better for me to be a stay-at-home mom, so after he got done with training, that's what happened."

"Did you like being a stay-at-home mom?" Tanner asks.

My shoulders shrug. "I liked the time I got to spend watching my kid grow and learn every day, but I'm also someone who enjoys getting out of the house. And I like having a job to go to where I make my own money. Kudos to those women who can do it, but I just don't think I was cut out for it. Staying home was way harder than any job I ever had. Once Alex was born, we were having trouble making ends meet, so I had to go back to work."

"Judd hated it. He believed that women belonged at home in the kitchen, not in the workforce. He watched all of his cop buddies come home to wives who were so perfect they put June Cleaver to shame while I would come home after work and whip together whatever was easiest. He would complain about the cooking constantly or that the house wasn't clean enough. Then, after Joey was born, it was all about my weight. With the other two kids, I lost my baby pounds pretty quickly, but after Joey, it was way harder, and I was too exhausted to spend every waking moment at the gym. The little bit of free time that I did have was spent cooking or cleaning instead of spending time with the kids. Judd got to do all the fun stuff while I had to be Zombie Mom."

Tanner interrupts. "That's bullshit."

"Which part?" I ask.

"I may not know much about marriage, but I know that it should be a partnership, not a constant weight on your shoulders while he gets to play good cop."

"That's what I was always taught, too," I tell him. "But Judd was raised in a very conservative family. All of the women stayed home cooking and pushing out babies, all while looking like they just stepped out of a magazine. I was never going to be that girl, and it pissed him off that he saw all of his cop buddies living out his dream. Over the years, it seemed like I put in more and more effort, but he saw it as me just getting worse. He took pleasure in telling me how unhappy he was with every little thing. Heaven forbid I burn dinner or forget to roll the garbage can to the curb. I would be hearing about it for the next week. I stuck it out as long as I could. I came from divorced parents, and I didn't want to do that to my own kids, but the situation eventually became so toxic that I filed for divorce."

"I bet that went over like a lead balloon."

"Oh yeah," I laugh. "He was so mad, but I took the boys and moved in with my dad. The divorce hearings were short because I told him he could have everything except for the kids. He tried to fight it, but I think it was just to spite me. He doesn't want three kids full time. That would take away his ability to be the fun dad. Even divorced, he still finds ways to make my life miserable. I think I'm doing just fine, and then, he makes some off-handed comment about the way that I look or how I take care of the house, and I'm right back in that place, listening to him complain and hoping that he will get over it soon."

Switching to rub my other foot, Tanner says, "For what it's worth, I think you're doing a great job."

There's no way he can possibly actually know that, but it's sweet of him to say nevertheless. "Thanks. It's taken a while, but I have slowly been able to relax. I realize that I no longer have to try to clean my house until it's spotless instead of spending time with my kids. And I no longer have to try to make myself look presentable for a man who thinks I'm hideous."

Tanner shakes his head back and forth. "I'm sorry, but if a woman carried three of my babies in her body, I would treat her like she was the most beautiful woman in the world."

"I guess stretchmarks and a big scar didn't do it for Judd."

Wiggling up and down his eyebrows, Tanner says, "Well, they sure as shit do it for me."

I want to tell him that I think he's full of crap and telling me what I want to hear, but I don't. I just smile and say, "Why don't you show me how much they do it for you?"

His tongue licks his bottom lip. "Gladly."

Each of his hands grab the sides of my face and pull me in for a kiss. The way his tongue lightly flicks against mine sets me ablaze.

"Come here," he commands, turning me so that my back is pressed against his chest. The moment I'm comfortable, his hands start to explore my body. Goosebumps erupt on my skin as he whispers in my ear. "Do you know how hard it is to sit across from you all naked and wet and keep my hands to myself?"

"Who says I want you to keep them to yourself?"

His fingers begin to toy with my nipples. As he teases them, my clit pulses, silently begging to be touched. How is it that this man knows just how to touch me to make me completely come unglued?

One of his hands move from my breast to between my legs. He slowly spreads my lower lips, giving the sensitive area time to get used to the hot water before starting to rub my clit. The moment his finger touches it, I let out a soft moan.

"Fuck, Erin," he whispers. "I love playing with this pussy."

"Yeah," I say breathlessly. "I love it too."

"Do you want me to make it come?" he asks.

I nod so hard I look like a dang bobblehead doll.

"Tell me what feels good, beautiful. I want to hear what you like. Every moan. Every whimper. Everything."

He doesn't have to tell me twice. I don't think I could control the sounds I'm making right now even if I tried.

I can't really see what he's doing to me, but it feels like he's holding my clit, lightly squeezing it between two fingers while rubbing the middle with his other one. I have no clue how he's doing it, but I don't care.

Keep doing your vagina sorcery, Mr. Samson.

I love it.

Suddenly, the water feels a lot hotter than it did just a few minutes ago.

"Oh, fuck," I moan. "Right there. Holy shit."

Motherhood has tamed my mouth down quite I bit. I try to watch the cursing, but when Tanner starts touching me, I turn into a sailor on leave.

I have no idea how long my orgasm takes because my brain seems to have gone on vacation for the moment, but eventually, I find myself teetering on the edge. My fingers grip into Tanner's thighs as I try to hold onto any semblance of control I have.

But when Tanner increases his tempo a little and whispers in my ear. "Come for me," I realize that any control I thought I had was clearly all in my head. Because my orgasm hits me hard. Water sloshes all over the place as I struggle to sit still.

He holds me tight until I finally start to settle. He leans in to say, "You look so fucking sexy when you come."

I could get used to this; Tanner is amazing.

But I know better than that.

This is temporary. It's just like one of the romance books I read.

A wonderful escape, but not reality.

Chapter Eleven

TANNER

"Are you ready for this cinematic masterpiece?" I ask Erin, who already doesn't look impressed.

She clicks the play button on the remote as she reads the title. "The Lord of the Rings: The Fellowship of the Ring. Is this a movie about a bunch of dudes fighting over some jewelry?"

"Well...technically, yes. But there's a whole lot more to it than that. There are orcs and hobbits and wizards."

"Oh my," she says sarcastically. "You're lucky you're a wizard in the bedroom. You make me come, and then, in my post-orgasm haze, you get me to agree to watch extremely long movies with you."

I grab her by the chin and pull her close. "How about we watch for a little while and then I do some more sex wizard stuff to your naked body?"

"You know I can't say no to that," she says with a grin.

The movie starts to play, and Erin watches intently as everything is explained. When I suggested we watch this, I wasn't one hundred percent serious, but she agreed, and I wasn't about to turn down a chance to watch it with her.

Our condoms arrived a few minutes ago, but I figure we can wait a little while before breaking into them. As much as I want to constantly bury myself inside Erin's sweet pussy, I equally want to spend some more time getting to know her.

I was surprised earlier when she opened up so much to me about her marriage and subsequent divorce. I tried to keep my cool while she talked, but it was hard as hell to keep my mouth shut about her shitty ex-husband.

That asshole had the nerve to tell her she wasn't sexy anymore after she carried three of his kids for nine months each? Fuck that.

Maybe it stems from my childhood, but I believe women should be treated like fucking queens. No matter how long I'm with a woman—whether it's one night or a whole year—I make sure they know how amazing they are.

Growing up, I saw my momma get with every lowlife in the area. She was a magnet for men who treated her like shit. I watched her heart get broken over and over again. I refuse to ever let any woman I ever date feel like that.

Any woman I am with will not be my maid or my mother—nor will I treat her as such. She will be my partner. If anything, I would take the brunt of things so she doesn't have to.

And I don't consider myself some sort of saint for that. I just consider myself a decent human being.

I'm sure most women look at me, and at first glance don't think I would be that type of man. They probably take one look at the long hair (and occasional man bun) and tattoos and think I'm automatically a douche bag.

But if they give me a chance, I do my best to prove them wrong. It can sometimes be hard when I have a job that has me on the road so much. That just means that I have to try that much harder when I'm home.

Best believe that if someone as amazing as Erin was home waiting for me every night, I would make sure that she felt as loved and appreciated as possible. Hell, I've only known her 24 hours, and I'm determined to still make her feel special.

Doesn't that sound ridiculous?

Twenty-four hours.

That's the blink of an eye in the grand scheme of things. But in those twenty-four hours, Erin and I have gotten to know each other just as much as we would if we'd gone on a few dates. And I've figured out that I like her...a lot.

I know she said she wasn't looking for anything serious, but man, I hope she changes her mind. I'm not sure if I could be the man that she needs although I'd love to try. If she tells me tomorrow that she never wants to see me again, I will respect that decision. Erin has much more to her life than just me, and I don't want to mess any of that up.

I run my fingers through her hair as the movie continues to play. Charlie gets up on the couch and lays behind her legs with his head on her butt, using it as a pillow.

I get it, boy. I like her butt, too.

Erin lets out a soft snore, and I realize I've lost her. Maybe Lord of the Rings wasn't the best option to start with. I have to admit that it moves a little slower than some of the other options.

I try to get as comfortable as possible without waking her up. As I stretch my legs out onto the coffee table, I notice a book sitting next to them. I assume it's one of Erin's dirty girl books.

What gave it away? The shirtless man on the cover?

Carefully, I reach forward and grab it. Quickly reading the back, I learn it's about a couple exploring their sexuality in an underground sex club.

Kinky.

Growing more intrigued by the second, I open the book to the page that is marked by a bookmark with puppies on it. Still trying to be quiet, my eyes begin to scan the page.

The entire room watches as I slowly take off my clothes, but the only thing I notice is Brett staring at me. It's like we are the only two in the room.

He sits in an armchair across from me, still fully dressed while I no longer have a scrap of clothing on—aside from my black stilettos.

"Open your legs," he commands.

I do as he says, the cool air hitting my wet center.

"Play with your pussy," he instructs. "I want you to make yourself come in front of all these people."

Holy shit.

This is what women read about in romance books?

Before I know it, I'm five pages in on a whole scene about this woman making herself orgasm in a room full of strangers. Whatever hope I had of not getting a boner is long gone because all I can think about is having Erin do this. She already told me that she reads this stuff and then makes herself come. Now, more than ever, I'd love to help her reenact some of this.

Maybe not the part about being in a room full of people who are watching. It's one thing to be surrounded by people and doing things to each other in secret. It's another to let a whole room full of people see her pussy. I don't consider myself jealous, but I don't know that I'm that understanding either.

I look at the title of the book again and make sure to remember to pick up my own copy. Maybe I'll read it right along with her and use it to turn her on like crazy.

My phone vibrates on the table next to me, and I about jump out of my skin. Erin stirs a little but doesn't wake up. I grab it and see that it's a text from my brother, Devon.

Devon: Hey dude, you okay?

Me: Yeah. Why?

Devon: I didn't hear from you after I left the bar last night. I went by your place, but you weren't there.

Me: Ended up meeting someone. Spending the weekend with her.

Devon: A whole weekend with a girl you just met? Man, she must be smokin' hot.

Man, he's got a lot of nerve, busting my balls.

Me: So, how's Kyra?

Devon: Not talking to me. Go figure.

Me: You know, there are actual women out there who will like you all the time...not just when it's convenient for them.

Devon: Yeah, where's the fun in that?

Me: I have to go, but I'll hit you up tomorrow when I'm home.

I set my phone back on the table and turn it on Do Not Disturb, so we don't have any more interruptions. My brothers and I are different as can be when it comes to love, but we all have the same core value of treating women like fucking queens.

Thankfully, Duke found Avery, who has been able to get him through all of the trauma that the SEALS caused him throughout the years.

Devon, on the other hand, has an innate ability to find women who treat him like shit. He puts them on a pedestal, and they don't return the favor. He loves Kyra to the moon and back, but I doubt she'd go even half as far for him.

And then, there's me. A guy who loves love and who would move heaven and hell to make his woman happy. But because of my job and as much as I travel, things tend not to work out. I refuse to stop trying, though.

The movie continues to play, and soon enough, I find my eyelids getting heavy. I look down at Erin who is still snoring and Charlie, who has passed out too.

Maybe the two of them have the right idea.

I have no idea how long I fall asleep for, but I'm more than thrilled to wake up when I feel something warm and wet wrapped around my cock.

My eyes spring open, and I look down to see Erin on her knees between my legs. I don't know how hard I had to be sleeping not to feel her moving around or pulling my dick out of my boxers. But there is nothing better in this world than waking up to a beautiful woman blowing you.

She looks up at me with her gray eyes. Her tongue swirls around the head like a lollipop as she asks, "Is this okay?"

"Are you kidding me? It's fucking perfect."

Her head bobs back down as she takes me as far into her mouth as she can. I feel the head hitting the back of her throat. She moves slowly, but I feel like it's more to tease me than anything.

"Fuck, Erin," I hiss through gritted teeth. "That feels so damn good."

For just a moment, I pull her off of me so that I can yank her t-shirt over her head. I want to see those big tits and sexy ass of hers.

My hand reaches down to play with her nipples while she gets back to work. Her nails lightly tickle my balls, and it takes every ounce of willpower I have not to come. When she hollows out her cheeks and sucks harder, I have to pull her off me once again to keep myself from blowing.

As much as I would love to come down her throat, I want to fuck her more.

Grabbing her arms, I pull her to her feet. "Get on the couch," I tell her. "Bend over with that sexy ass in the air."

Quickly, I run off to the kitchen to grab the condoms on the counter. Multi-tasking, I roll the rubber on as I run back. I stop dead in my tracks at seeing that juicy ass of hers in the air, waiting for me.

I walk over to her and rub the soft cheeks before moving down to her pussy. My finger swipes through her slit to make sure she's ready for me.

"Already so wet," I tell her before replacing my finger with my cock.

I start slowly as not to give her too much at once, but that doesn't last long. When she uses her ass to push back against me at the speed that she wants it, my resolve breaks, and I start to pound into her.

Her moans echo off the walls while my eyes stay glued to her ass. I love the way it bounces as I fuck her.

"Oh, fuck!" She cries.

I love hearing her dirty little mouth when I'm inside her. She goes from all sugar to all spice in about ten seconds.

And I can't seem to get enough.
How am I supposed to walk away from this tomorrow?

97

Chapter Twelve

"Oh, no," Tanner says, shaking his head. "We can't have that. Lay down. We will take care of this right now."

I let out a soft laugh. "Tanner, it's fine. I take longer to come. It's completely normal that I don't get off every single time I have sex."

He's still shaking his head. "Sweetheart, let me tell you something. Even if I can't get you off during sex, I sure as hell am going to get you off in other ways. It's not fair that I got to come and you didn't."

This whole thing is so new for me. With Judd, he didn't really care if I got off or not. He thought a man coming was more of a "need" while a woman coming was more a "bonus". On special occasions, he would take the time to make sure I had an orgasm. But other than that, he didn't care.

And here Tanner is feeling bad that he didn't get me off. He's made me come more this weekend than

Judd did in the last few years of my marriage. How sad is that?

Tanner pulls his hair back into a small bun before starting to make his way between my legs, but I grab his face to stop him.

"Fabio, as much as I want you to do that some more, I'm going to need some food."

His face falls a little, and I can tell that he still feels bad. It really is unnecessary, though. The sex was still fantastic. It felt incredible, and no way am I complaining.

"Fine," he pouts. "But later on, I'm making you come twice. No! Three times!"

"Oh, no!" I joke while throwing my hands up. "Threatening me with orgasms."

Fifteen minutes later, Tanner is standing at my stove making fajitas. The smell of steak, onions, and peppers fills the air, and my mouth waters. Have I mentioned how sexy he looks cooking for me? I make sure to take a mental picture since I doubt I'll see it again any time soon.

"Who taught you how to cook?" I ask. "Your mom?"

He throws his head back and laughs. "No. Definitely not my mom. She was the kind of mom who burned toast every time she tried to make it."

"So, where did you learn?"

He looks at me and gives a crooked smile. "You'll laugh."

"Try me."

"When I first started the job I'm at, I found myself eating fast food constantly. When I was on the road,

I was eating at every greasy restaurant you can imagine. And when I'd come home, I didn't know how to cook shit, so I ate a lot of the same. After a while, I just got sick of it. It was making me feel like crap, so I decided to learn how to cook. That way, at least when I'm home, I know that I can have a good meal."

I listen to his story and narrow in my eyes at him. "That doesn't really answer my question. You answered *why* you learned how to cook but not how."

He rolls his eyes and sighs. "I watched a whole lot of Gordon Ramsay videos on YouTube, okay?"

I make good on my promise and don't laugh at him. "Hey, I think if you are going to learn how to cook, why not learn to cook from the best?"

His lips pull into a big grin, showing his mouthful of pearly whites. "That was my thinking exactly."

"I love watching all of his cooking shows while I make dinner. Well, the ones where he yells at people. The ones where he is nice just don't hold my interest."

He nods. "Same. It was a little weird following the tutorials and not hearing him call me a donkey along the way."

"Tell me more about your mom," I say, hoping to gleam more of what makes Tanner Samson tick.

"Tammy Samson is a character," he says, looking up at me while he stirs everything in the skillet. "She's the epitome of unlucky in love. She's been married a handful of times, engaged just as many, and dated more than that. It was never that she was a bad mom, but motherhood took a backseat to her love life."

"That sounds rough," I say.

"Honestly, my brothers probably had it worse than I did. My oldest brother is about fifteen years older than me, and the other one is right in the middle of us. They both probably got it worse than I did. By the time I came around, she was a bit more stable. That's probably why the other two hold more resentment toward her than I do, especially Duke, my oldest brother. He and Momma went round and round for years. They've made amends recently, but it was bad for a while."

"Are you close to your brothers?"

He shrugs. "Pretty close, I guess. Closer to Devon than to Duke just because we were closer in age. Duke joined the military when I was like three years old, so he wasn't around much while I was growing up. But we all try to hang out when we can. What about you? Any siblings?"

"I have an older brother, Wes. But he lives in Arizona now, so we don't see him much. We still talk sometimes, but we aren't close."

"And your parents?"

"Divorced," she says. "My mom remarried a while ago and moved to California. My dad is still local, though, and he's my kids' absolutely favorite person."

"That's awesome." He smiles. "I'm pretty sure my momma is slowly giving up hope of any of us giving her grandbabies."

"You don't want kids?" I ask. My stomach clenches as I wait for his answer, though I have no idea why. Why should I care if this guy wants kids or not? After tomorrow, he will be a distant memory.

I can say those words all that I want, but I can't deny the little voice in my head telling me that this is something more than just a two-and-a-half-day fling.

That's just wishful thinking, though.

"I'd love to have kids," he replies, and I breathe a sigh of relief. "I love kids. Sometimes, my job just makes it hard to get close to people."

"What do you mean?"

"I mean some women aren't okay with the fact that I travel a lot. They may not entirely trust the decisions that I make when I'm away from them."

I'm not really sure what to say to that. The curiosity in me wants to just ask if there's any merit to that. But quite frankly, it's none of my business. Tanner doesn't seem like the type of man who would cheat, but I've known this guy for like a millisecond, so what do I know? It's like I have a great barometer for choosing men, either.

I decide just to keep my mouth shut, but apparently, my face gives me away.

"Just in case you're wondering, Erin, no, I haven't cheated on a woman when I'm on the road. I've never cheated on a woman period."

"I wasn't—" I stammer.

"It's alright." He gives me a reassuring smile. "It's a valid question."

"Must get lonely to be on the road that much," I say.

"Sometimes. But I mean, most of the time, I'm exhausted in the evenings. I usually work about twelve hours a day to try to stay ahead of schedule, so I pass out pretty early. Sometimes, if I'm single and horny, I'll go out for a while, but if I have someone waiting for me back home, no way."

"Sounds like you're a good man, Tanner Samson. Some woman is going to be very lucky to have you," I tell him.

"Thank you for that, gorgeous. But as far as I'm concerned that's the absolute least that a man should do. Being faithful should be a no-brainer."

Well, I guess it SHOULD be.

Tanner fixes us a couple of plates and takes them to the living room. We get comfortable around the coffee table and dig in.

"This is incredible," I tell him after the first bite.

"Glad you like it."

We eat in silence for a few minutes before he speaks again. "You said your mom lives in California?"

I give a slow nod. My mom is a bit of a touchy subject, but I've opened up about quite a bit of touchy subjects already, so why not?

"Yeah, when I was a teenager, she left my dad. She ran off with some guy she met on the internet."

"Ouch. Your dad got you in the divorce?"

"If you could call it that," I say. "She didn't want either of us. She just left us with nothing more than a note. My dad didn't get divorce papers until she wanted to get remarried."

"Has she ever apologized?"

"She's tried. But I refuse to talk to her. I think Wes listened to her whole speech, but I don't want to hear it. If she wanted a divorce, she could have done that without doing all the damage that she did." Looking at Tanner, I point at him and add, "Don't you dare tell me that I should try to make amends before it's too late or any of that other crap."

"Wouldn't dream of it." He takes a couple more bites before asking, "Do you think that going through that with your mom is part of the reason you stayed in your marriage for so long?"

Avoiding his eyes, I respond, "Probably. I'm sure it messed me up probably more than I even realize."

When we finish eating, I chug the rest of my margarita and scoot closer to him on the couch. "I feel like you're my therapist or something," I tell him. "I never open up to anyone."

"I'm always happy to listen, beautiful, but I'm fairly positive that it would be illegal for me to be your therapist and do the dirty things I'm about to do to you."

I lean in to kiss him. "Quit talking and show me."

Chapter Thirteen

ERIN

"You know, I'm getting pretty used to you being in here with me," I say, gesturing to the bathtub we are sitting in once again. "It's not going to be quite the same being in here by myself."

"How do you think I feel? I'm not going to see a beautiful naked woman sitting across from me, all soapy and wet."

"Oh, I'm sure you could easily find someone to take my place," I reply, a bit snarkier than I intend to.

His fingertips lightly rub along my knee that sticks out of the water. "Oh, beautiful, I don't think you're going to be nearly that easy to get over."

"It's only been a couple of days," I argue. "I'm sure you'll be fine."

He smiles at me. "Erin, I'm not saying I'm going to sit in the corner and cry about the girl who got away. But I don't think you give yourself enough credit for how fucking awesome you are."

I don't want to disagree with him, but I don't think there's anything overly special about me. I'm not trying to sell myself short, either. I think I'm a good person with a big heart, but I don't think I have a lot that will make men fall in love with me. Putting 'mom of three kids' on a dating profile isn't exactly a siren call to eligible men.

"What are you thinking about, beautiful?" Tanner asks.

"Just thinking about how life has a funny way of surprising you."

"What do you mean?"

"A couple years ago, I was married. My life looked totally different. I was constantly stressed and on edge, but every single day, I told myself that it would pass and that things would get better. Fast forward, and I get divorced. After the initial devastation wore off, I felt utter relief. And terror. Let's not forget terror. And now, I'm here with this gorgeous twenty-five-year-old man who is taking a bath with me. A couple years ago, if you would have told me that I'd be here right now, I would have thought you were crazy. It just makes me wonder what other surprises life has in store for me. Makes me wonder where my life is going from here."

"Where do you *want* it to go?" He asks.

I sit quietly for a moment because honestly, I don't know that I've thought about an answer to that question.

"Erin, you good?"

"Yeah, I just haven't really thought about it, I guess. Lately, I've been so busy just trying to get through one day at a time that I just focus on the now rather than worrying about the future."

"I feel that. What has been your dream? Like if you could do anything you wanted, what would it be?"

"Hmm." I tap my finger on the side of the tub. "I'm not sure. I mean, I don't mind my job. I love the people I work with, and the pay gets us by."

"Alright, what about outside of work? Anywhere you want to travel? Anything crazy you want to do?"

"That's a different story. I'd love to travel anywhere and everywhere. One regret that I think I'll always have is that I don't always have the money to take my kids to do all the fun things. It's hard to make memories on a single income. Even going to the zoo these days costs an arm and a leg."

"I can only imagine. It's just me, and for a while, it was hard to make ends meet." After a long pause he asks, "Have you ever thought about trying to sing professionally? You've got quite the set of pipes on you."

Just the thought of that makes my stomach twist into a knot. "Uhm no. Nope. No way. Definitely not."

Sarcastically, he asks, "So, that's a no?"

"The ONLY reason I was able to do karaoke was because I was drunk. Without alcohol, there's no way I could do. I have stage fright way too bad."

"You seemed right at home up there."

"Tequila is a wonderful liquid, my friend."

He laughs as his fingers massage my calves. "No joke. I should thank tequila because it got you to come home with me."

"You don't think you could have sealed the deal if I wasn't drunk?"

"I want to say yes, but I don't know if I'm that smooth."

"Are you kidding me, Fabio? You're smoother than a dolphin's belly."

His eyebrows furrow. "That's an *interesting* analogy."

"I still probably would have gone home with you if I wasn't all loaded up on margs." I say the words, but I'm not sure I know how true they are. I think that the tequila gave me just the amount of courage I needed to be able to let loose a little. I have no idea how I would have reacted if Tanner had hit on me while I was sober. I haven't had anyone really hit on me so long that I have no idea how I would react.

But I don't want to make Tanner feel bad because he really is smooth as sin, and I'm sure he could get any girl he wanted if he really tried... including me.

"There is one thing I always wanted to do," I tell him. "But it's silly."

"Tell me." he prompts.

"Back in the day, I used to want to write. I always told myself I would put out a romance book. I even used to write stories in notebooks all the time."

"Why didn't you ever pursue it?"

"Because Judd hated it. Told me that I would embarrass him if I put out any of that *romance trash*. And I just got too busy to even want to mess with it anymore."

Deciding to change the subject, I ask, "So, what do your tattoos mean?"

With a confident smile, he replies, "Not a damn thing."

"What do you mean? Don't people get tattoos based on some sort of deep meaning?"

"I'm sure a lot of people do. When I first started traveling, I was on the road a lot more than I am now. I was gone for sometimes three to four weeks at a time. That was a whole lot of time to kill in the evenings, so I would hit up the local tattoo shop of whatever town or city we were in. I'd walk up to the tattoo artist and tell them to give me whatever they wanted. I'd ask what their favorite tattoos to give were. Some of them gave me cool flowers. Some gave me simple designs. Others gave me intricate masterpieces. But I'd like to think that they're all a little special because the artist got to do a tattoo that they really and truly enjoyed doing."

Okay, put another tally in the column for this guy having an absolute heart of gold. I'm not sure I could make any of this up in my head if I tried.

"I think the fact that you did that gives all of your tattoos meaning—at least meaning to the artists who did them."

He gives a little shrug. "I guess so."

"I always kind of wanted one but never got around to it."

"Oh, trust me, beautiful; if you had a tattoo, I would have noticed. I made mental notes of every inch of your body. Why haven't you gotten one?"

I stifle the urge to tell him that Judd thought they looked trashy, and I didn't need one more reason for him to find me hideous.

Instead, I just say, "Just never got around to it, I suppose."

His eyes squint the slightest bit like he wants to ask more, but he resists. "Maybe we can go get you one sometime."

There's a loud screaming voice in my head telling me that there will be no tattoo getting because this little fling isn't going to last past later on today. As wonderful as this has been, it's fleeting.

And because I'm just not able to help myself, I say, "Unless we go get one in the next couple hours, I don't think that's going to happen."

Why am I like this? Why do I have to ruin this great moment?

"Erin, I know you said this weekend was all you could offer. I respect that, but I also am curious as to why. I get that you're a mom, and you're probably busier than I can imagine. But it seems like there's more to it than that."

I let out a heavy sigh. "Judd and I agreed not to bring relationships around our kids as to not mess them up any more than we probably already have. And even though I don't have them every other weekend, I don't think that's enough time to make a relationship work."

He nods. "Trust me. I get it. Growing up, I saw way too many guys come and go. It wasn't an ideal situation."

We both fall silent because neither of us quite know what to say. I wish things could be different. I wish I could spend all of my free weekends half-naked and in his arms. But that's not fair to him. Relationships aren't built on only four days a month.

He says, "I guess we better make the most of the few hours that we have left, huh?"

A big smile tugs at the corners of my lips. "I guess so."

With his finger under my chin, he pulls me toward him for a long, sensual kiss. I swear his tongue makes my head spin.

Everything that he does with his tongue.

Just when I start to get lost in the moment, he stops and suggests we move this out of the tub. With a completely hard cock, he stands up and reaches for my hand. He steps out first, and quickly wraps a towel around his waist before taking the time to dry off every inch of me.

When he's done, he leads me to the bedroom and tells me to lie down. I do as he says and patiently wait. My entire body practically buzzes with excitement, waiting to see what he has planned.

My excitement grows when I see his head duck between my thighs.

He whispers, "Do you know how much I love eating this pussy?"

Feeling bold, I reply, "Show me."

As if I hit some magical switch inside of Tanner, he starts licking me like it's the last thing he will ever do. His tongue makes sure to give every inch of me its attention all while making his main focus my clit. Just when he starts licking my clit to a point where I think I'm going to come, he eases back and lets my body relax. It's driving me crazy but making for one heck of a buildup.

"Tanner," I plead, anxious for some release.

He stops licking long enough to say, "Tell me what you want."

"Make me come. Please," I beg.

He slips two fingers inside my pussy and angles them to play with that magical spot inside me while his tongue goes back to licking my clit. To add a new twist to the mix, I feel his pinky rubbing the sensitive area around my asshole. I've never done any type of anal play, but I've read about it in my books and always wanted to try.

I feel him slip his finger in the tiniest bit, and I try to relax. It's hard though when my entire body is practically shaking as I feel my orgasm looming. When he sucks my clit between his teeth while he continues to lick, I'm done.

I scream a slew of obscenities, but I'm so deep in the pleasure I have no idea what I'm even saying. My thighs clench, and my fingers fist in Tanner's hair as I come for what feels like an eternity.

Before I even have a chance to recover, he's already gotten up to slip a condom on and is back between my legs. He seems to do it at lightning speed. Or maybe I'm just so out of it, I have no concept of time.

Wrapping one of my legs around his waist, he slides inside. We've had a decent amount of sex this weekend, but this time feels different.

Not only do I know it's our last time, but it *feels* like our last time.

If things were different, I could see me getting serious with someone like Tanner. Despite the age difference, I think we would be great together. It's clear that we both feel that, but instead of saying it, we pour every emotion into making this last time special.

Every kiss.

Every touch.

Every movement.

It's all filled with passion and heat. We are locked in this perfect moment, forgetting about everything else in the world and focusing on just us. I'm even almost able to forget about the fact that this will never happen again.

Almost.

Chapter Fourteen

TANNER

"Come on," Erin pleads. "Please let me drive you. It's really not a big deal. Let me find my keys."

Grabbing her by the hand, I pull her toward me, pressing my lips to hers to quiet her. When I pull back, I say, "Hey, it's alright. A walk will do me some good."

"But you have to walk all the way to the bar."

I laugh. "Erin, we could fit the entire town of Maple Oaks in a shoebox. It will take me ten minutes, fifteen tops."

She pouts. "I just feel bad."

"Don't," I say, giving her another kiss. "I could use the fresh air. Plus, it will give you a little more alone time before the kids come home."

She still isn't completely sold on the idea, but she doesn't press any further.

It's still a couple hours until she said her kids were coming home, and as much as I would love to stay and continue to do dirty things to her., I don't want to risk her kids coming home early. I don't think that would go over too well with anyone involved.

I thought about trying to convince her to give this thing between us a shot, but I can tell she already feels bad, and I don't want to make it worse. She has her reasons for doing what she's doing, and I intend to respect that—no matter how much it sucks.

I watch as she fiddles with her hands and bites her fingernails. The woman in front of me is far different than the one I saw in the bar Friday night, but to me, she's just as beautiful. Her hair is piled in a bun on top of her head, and she wears thick black-rimmed glasses. That ex-husband of hers is a dirtbag for ever thinking that this woman isn't amazing. I would consider myself one lucky son-of-a-bitch to wake up to her like this every single morning.

Walking over to the coffee table, I grab my phone and slide it into my pocket. It feels a little odd wearing this much clothing after being practically naked all weekend long. Checking to make sure I have everything, I figure it's about time for me to be heading out.

With a shaky voice, Erin begins to speak. "Tanner, I just need you to know..."

I stop her. "Hey, you don't have to say anything."

"No. I want to." She pauses before continuing. "I had no idea what I was doing when I asked you to come home with me Friday night. I was half convinced it would be a disaster, but you made me feel things that I haven't felt in a very long time. I can't tell you how much I appreciate that."

"You deserve to be shown those things every day," I tell her.

Her lip quivers, and her eyes well up with tears. "I really wish things could be different. I wish I could give you more, but I just don't think I can."

I kiss away the lone tear rolling down her cheek. "I know. How about I make you deal?"

She looks up at me, waiting for me to continue.

"I won't press for this to go any further, but if you ever find yourself lonely again on a weekend you don't have your kids, you can call, and I'll come running."

"Really?" She gives me a soft smile. "That wouldn't feel like I was using you?"

"Sweetheart, I would gladly get used by you any day of the week. And if you think I would give up a chance to get in between those luscious legs of yours, you're crazy."

Her smile grows, but I can still see the doubt on her face. I'd be surprised if I hear from her after today.

I grab a pen and scrap of paper off one of the end tables and jot my number down. "I'll leave this here just in case you need it. If you don't, that's okay too."

Pulling her close, I give her one final kiss. And to make sure she remembers me, I make it a good one.

When we finish, I say, "Maybe I'll see you around, beautiful."

Tears fill her eyes once again, and she nods as she walks me toward the door. I take one final look at her gorgeous face before walking through it.

The moment the door shuts behind me, I feel like the fantasy we've been living in all weekend is shattered. In a heartbeat, it's back to reality.

The Texas heat bears down on me as I make my way to the bar, but my mind is so filled with thoughts of Erin that I don't even notice. I'm basically on autopilot the entire way, not paying much attention to anything around me.

But when I finally arrive, I realize just how hot I actually am, so I decide to duck inside and grab a water real quick. When I enter, I'm surprised at who I see behind the bar. It looks like one of Erin's friends from the other night.

Not wanting to make anything weird, I'm about to head back out without the water, but she sees me, and we make eye contact.

Well, there goes that idea.

The place is pretty empty, so I walk over and take a seat at one of the barstools.

"You're Erin's friend, right?" I ask.

She nods. "Gina. Should I be worried that you're here, and I haven't heard from her?"

"I just left her house," I tell her.

Her eyes narrow in on me. "That doesn't answer my question."

"She was good. We had a great weekend together, but she told me it couldn't continue on."

She fills up a pint glass with a draft beer and hands it to me. "On the house."

I didn't plan on having anything except water, but I'm not going to turn down a free beer.

Gina lets out a loud sigh. "I was hoping she'd be able to get over that stupid agreement she had with Judd. Heaven knows he's probably not sticking to his end of the deal."

"Have you told her that?" I ask.

"Not in so many words. Erin will take a lot of shit from a lot of people, but when it comes to anything having to do with her being a momma, she will cut your heart clean out of your chest. I support her however I can. Sometimes, that means keeping my mouth shut about the person she chose to father her children with."

I take a sip of beer before saying, "I'm pretty crazy about her, but I'm with you on the not pushing her thing."

She leans against the bar. "I really thought that having some fun would make her see that she can still have a life while being a mom."

I really have no idea what to say, so I just nod.

Another customer gets her attention, but before Gina walks away, she said, "Maybe she will change her mind."

Lord, I hope so.

Chapter Fifteen

ERIN

"Momma, can I play on your phone?" Joey asks me for the fifth time today.

Earlier, I had the energy to keep telling him no, but right now, I'd give anything for him to just sit still. So, I hand him my phone and tell him he has to sit on his butt, or the phone comes back to me. The past half an hour has been spent with him running up and down the bleachers, and me convinced that he's going to break his neck.

Why can't school sporting events ever start on time?

Chris sits a couple feet away from us, as though he's far too cool to be seen with his mom and little brother.

The only thing I get from him is a loud sigh and him saying, "When is this stupid soccer game going to start? I'm bored."

"Chris, we literally watch you play every sport under the sun. It won't kill you to sit here a little bit longer," I tell him.

Thankfully, he goes back to ignoring me and playing on his own phone, letting me get back to the fantasy playing out in my head. It's been a few days since I told Tanner goodbye, but I still can't seem to get him out of my head. I find myself wondering where he's working or how he's doing... but most of all, I remember all the dirty things he did to me.

All of the mundane things that I do on a day-to-day basis are now a bit more exciting when my daydreams take hold.

Folding laundry? Thinking about Tanner going down on me.

Cleaning the toilet? Picturing Tanner pounding me from behind.

Driving to sports practice? Playing out some of the scenes in my books with Tanner as the leading character.

I've never been so horny in all my life. I've always liked sex, but it's always been something that I can take or leave. It wasn't any type of highlight for me.

Now, that I've had *good* sex, though, I realize exactly what I've been missing. And boy, oh boy, I sure am missing it.

The moment Tanner left the other night, the dam opened, and all my tears came out in full force. Saying goodbye to him was more difficult than I ever thought it could be—which is ridiculous because we knew each other all of 48 hours.

How crazy does that sound?

Nevertheless, I was sad about losing what *could have been,* I guess.

I'm still sad about the entire situation, but now, something else has joined the party.

Horniness.

Each night, my vibrator is getting more of a workout than it's gotten in years. Sure, I will read my books and use it every now and then, but now, I'm touching myself like a guy who just discovered porn.

Even when I read all the sexy stuff in my romance novels now, all I can picture is Tanner doing those things to me.

I bet he'd be good at all of them.

I figure as time goes on, Tanner will slowly start to fade from my mind. I mean, he has to, right? I can't go on pining for this man forever.

Gina called me yesterday to see how everything went over the weekend and then asked a bunch of questions that I didn't want to hear—mainly because I have no idea how to answer them.

Are you really going to be alone until all your kids are out of the house? You realize Joey is only four? That's fourteen more years of you putting everyone else ahead of yourself.

How long are you going to let Judd have control over what you do in YOUR life?

Don't you want your kids to see their mother be HAPPY?

The whole thing felt like I was being attacked at the time, but since I've had to think about it, I know she's just looking out for me. That doesn't make it any easier to hear, though. Because honestly, I don't have an answer to any of it.

Although I haven't thought much about actually being with somebody seriously, I hadn't considered the fact that Judd and my agreement means I wouldn't be with anyone for a huge chunk of my life. And I already feel like I wasted so much of it with Judd, I'm not sure how much more I want to give up.

I don't know. I don't have any answers. All I know is that I'm the rock that my kids depend on. Right now, that should be my focus.

With the occasional daydream about Tanner to get me through.

Pulling me from my thoughts, Chris asks, "Is Dad still coming?"

"I think so," I tell him. "Maybe he got held up at work."

I have to give Judd credit that he makes an effort to come to most of the kids' games and tries to make to the practices that I can't make it to. With two kids in sports full time and one just starting out, it takes both of us to figure out a good schedule. It's quite possibly the one thing Judd and I can be civil on.

It is a little surprising that he's not here yet. I consider texting him, but he would probably just give me crap about not leaving him alone, so I decide against it.

A few minutes later, the game starts, and I watch all the kids kick the ball back and forth—and kick it out of bounds approximately every six seconds. They're eight and not great at ball control.

Joey suddenly cries, "Dad's here!"

I look over to see Judd walking toward the bleachers.

And he's not alone.

Pure shock overcomes me as I see him holding hands with a long-legged blonde woman. With her painted-on makeup and big hair, she looks like she's ready to compete in a Dolly Parton look alike contest.

I shouldn't say that.

Dolly Parton is far too classy to be in a category with this woman, look alike or not.

Just when I think my shock level couldn't be any higher, Joey yells, "Mary Louise!" As he runs over to see her and his daddy.

I'm sorry. Do my kids KNOW this woman?

"Hey there, JoJo," she says in her sweeter than sweet tea accent.

JoJo? Are you kidding me? Who does this woman think she is?

As they get closer, the woman sees Chris sitting by me and puts two and two together on who I am.

"You must be Erin!" She croons. "I've been itching to meet you for a while now."

"Hi," is all I can manage to get out.

She puts her hand over her chest, showing off her long, fake nails. "I'm Mary Louise."

Judd can clearly see the befuddled look on my face and says, "Hey, honey, why don't we go sit up top?"

She playfully smacks his shoulder. "Oh, no way! We aren't going to leave Erin down here all by herself."

Please don't.

Before I can say a word, she's taken a seat next to me and said, "This way, Erin and I can get to know each other better."

So, not only did Judd break our deal about not seeing other people, but he's clearly brought her around our kids before. And now, he's bringing her to soccer games and letting her sit next to me.

What is happening?

Thankfully, Joey does most of the talking and keeps Miss Pageant Queen amused. I try to turn my focus back to the game, but it's hard. All of my shock has been replaced with pure rage. I've been so worried about breaking this stupid pact with Judd to try to do what was best for our kids. Meanwhile, he didn't give a crap about any of it.

I practically told Tanner to get lost because I thought I was doing what I was *supposed* to. And for what? For Judd to show up to our kid's soccer game with his new woman in tow.

When Joey finally comes up for air, Mary Louise turns toward me and says, "So, Erin Judd tells me you work at some sort of doctors office?"

Without looking at her, I respond with, "A dentist office actually."

Like Judd doesn't know that. My job is too insignificant for him to even accurately describe it to others.

She says, "Oh, well that sounds exciting!"

She doesn't say it with an ounce of condescension but more like she's actually interested. I can't tell if she's just super nice or if she's putting on the best front I've ever seen.

I really want to respond with some sarcastic answer, but with my kids right here, I decide to be the bigger person.

"What do you do for work, Mary Louise?"

"Oh, I don't work anymore." She turns toward Judd. "Not since I moved in with this guy."

Okay, I'm going to be sick. Physically ill.

Thankfully, the whistle blows, signaling halftime. I turn toward Judd, "Can I talk to you for a second?"

He rolls his eyes and gives a heavy sigh, making his annoyance known, but he still follows me.

When we are out of earshot of everyone else, I say, "When did you start dating?"

The crease in his forehead appears—the crease he gets every time he has to interact with me. "I started dating Mary Louise a couple months ago, but I guess I've been dating in general since about a month or so after the divorce was finalized."

"I'm sorry, what?" I ask. "What happened to you and I not dating anyone to make things easier on our kids? We weren't going to just bring around a bunch of randoms."

"And I haven't." He says the words as though I'm stupid. "Mary Louise isn't a random. We live together now, so the kids were bound to meet her. It's pretty serious. Before that, I didn't bring home every woman that I took to bed."

It completely blows my mind that I have been worried about the ONE guy I was with for ONE weekend, yet apparently, Judd has had a parade of women over the past year.

"That agreement was your idea," I say through gritted teeth.

"Erin, if we kept to that agreement, we would both be alone for the next fourteen years. Maybe that's okay with you, but I'd rather find someone who actually makes me happy. Someone who actually *wants* to be a wife."

With that, he walks away.

The pit in my stomach starts to form again. Judd doesn't want a wife. He wants a maid, a personal chef, and a woman who says yes to whatever he says. Apparently, Mary Louise fits into that mold.

I manage to watch the rest of the soccer game without having to interact much with Judd's new girlfriend. Joey keeps her pretty well amused. I make a mental note to let him have some extra ice cream for dessert tonight for helping me dodge that bullet.

When the game is over, and the boys and I are safely in my SUV, I pause before starting it.

Turning toward my children, I take a deep breath before beginning. "I know I don't often talk like this, so forgive me...but what the fuck?"

They all look shocked at me dropping the F-bomb. Joey even audibly gasps. Without giving them the chance to say anything, I start talking again. "Why would you guys not give me some sort of heads up that your dad has a girlfriend that is *living with him?"*

Chris is the first to speak. "Dad told us not to."

Alex adds, "He thought you'd be mad."

My anger surges to new levels. If Judd didn't think he was doing anything wrong, why on Earth did he ask my children to lie to me? In all honesty, I can't be mad at the kids. They are between a rock and a hard place. And by all appearances, they seem to like Mary Louise.

Keeping that in mind, I try not to take my anger out on them. I take another deep breath, this time, it's in an attempt to keep my cool. "Look, I know you guys have a relationship with your dad, and I will always try to respect that. Just a little bit of heads-up would have been nice. We are all still adjusting to this whole situation, and we need to be on the same page. Okay?"

They all nod and give me a, "Sorry, Mom."

"It's okay," I tell them. "I don't like that you were put in this situation to start with."

I leave it at that because I don't want to say anything worse about their dad even though right now, I feel like I could spit nails. At the soccer fields, I wanted to give him all the hell he deserves, but there's still something inside me that tells me to keep me mouth shut and not make any waves.

I'm too tired to mess with making dinner tonight, so we stop at McDonalds, and I let the kids order whatever they want while I opt for a Big Mac and Fries. Clearly, it's not the best food, but it's good and comforting.

Thankfully, by the time we get home, it's time for showers and then for the kids to get into bed. I love my children to pieces, but right now, I need to be alone with my thoughts.

When I finally have the downstairs to myself, I decide to deep clean the kitchen. For whatever reason, when I'm irritated, cleaning helps me to try to collect my thoughts.

At least, it *normally* does.

Tonight, though, my mind is too frazzled to clean. Instead, I walk into the living room and call Charlie up to snuggle me on the couch.

A million thoughts run through my head. Seeing Judd with that woman didn't make me jealous in a sense of "man, I want him back." Make no mistake, I will *never* want that man back. The only thing I was jealous of was the fact that he is doing something that makes him happy.

Or *someone*, I guess.

Meanwhile, I had an amazing guy who *wanted* to have a relationship with me. Tanner practically begged me to give this thing a chance, and I shot it down because I was so worried about keeping the peace. And now, he's gone. I haven't heard from him since.

He's probably already moved on with some hottie who doesn't have a boat load of baggage.

Charlie sneezes, causing a piece of paper on the end table to go flying. When I reach down to pick it up, I see that it's Tanner's number that he wrote down for me. The other day, I was going to throw it away, but I just couldn't.

And now, somehow, here it is...seemingly at the exact time that I need it. I twirl the tiny piece of paper between my fingers, trying to figure out if I should call him. If I believed in divine intervention, I'd say this is as good of a sign as any. But I'm still not entirely sure.

It's not like I have any idea how to do a relationship while also doing the mom thing, and I will probably mess it up one way or another. I would be in no hurry for him to meet my kids, so it's not like I could give him more than a couple weekends a month.

I have no idea how long I sit, trying to figure out what I should do. Finally, I muster all the courage that I possibly can and pull out my phone.

Here we go.

Chapter Sixteen

TANNER

"Can I get you anything else, sweetheart?" The bartender asks.

"No, thanks. I think I'm good."

She walks away, looking a little irritated that I'm not ordering more than one drink and a burger. I make a mental note to leave her a hell of a tip. If I'm taking up a barstool, I'm going to make it worth her time.

Work went a little later than I thought it would tonight, so I decided to just hit up the bar that's in the lobby of my hotel. Usually, we stay in crappy motels, so I take advantage when I can.

My gaze is fixed on the basketball game on the TV, so I don't even notice when a woman sits down next to me.

"You here alone?" She asks in a sultry voice.

Looking over at her, I see that she's definitely a looker. I can tell that she came out today with the goal of taking someone home. Under normal circumstances, I would probably be that guy.

But not tonight.

Tonight, I'm just not feeling it.

Not wanting to think that there's anything wrong with her, I turn to the woman next to me and say, "I'm actually on my way to meet my girl now."

I stand up and walk out of the bar and back into the lobby of the hotel. My eyes glance over to the elevator before looking at the time. As tired as I may be, I don't think I'm ready to call it a night just yet.

I'm on the outskirts of downtown Houston, so there has to be something around here I can do. I walk down the street for a while until I come across a bookstore. Typically, I would never just walk into a bookstore, but this one, is cute and quaint... and reminds me of Erin.

I have no idea why. It just looks like somewhere that she would like.

Despite my best efforts, I haven't been able to get her out of my head. Well, I guess I could try harder. Going home with the stunner from the bar probably would have been a good start. In fact, I have had the chance to go home with a couple of different women over the past few days, but none of it has felt right. I'm sure soon enough, my dick will get horny enough to want to get into something, but right now, I'm just fine with rubbing one out, thinking about Erin's ass bouncing as I fuck her from behind.

Lord, I sound pathetic. I'm pining for a girl that I had a fun weekend with.

It doesn't help that Erin wasn't just some girl I met in a bar—well, okay, I guess she was. But she was also someone I could see spending my life with. She actually had something to say.

The moment I walk into the store, the woman at the counter greets me with a, "What brings you in today?"

I feel a little awkward, but I still respond with, "I'm looking for the romance section."

She just points to the way and tells me which aisle I'm looking for before going back to tagging the large stack of books in front of her. I don't know why I was expecting more of a reaction. Maybe she gets a lot of guys coming in here, asking for romance books. I mean, honestly, guys probably *should* come here and read some of these books. One, what a great place to meet women. And two, you get a basic manual on what women like.

The first romance section that I come to looks like the kind I would see my momma reading. They all look like they're more on the historical side. Finally, I get to a section labeled #**smut**. I'm guessing I'm in the right spot.

I browse for a minute before a cover catches my eye. It's the same one that Erin was reading, and I discover it's part of a set.

Without even thinking about it, I pick up all the books in the series and take them to the counter. If I can't have Erin, I can at least do something to make me feel closer to her.

Lord, I'm glutton for punishment.

I head back to my hotel room and get comfortable on the bed, ready to settle in with one of these good books.

Just when I'm a couple chapters in. My phone rings, and it's a Maple Oaks phone number, so I decide to answer. "Hello?"

There is only silence for a moment before the phone goes dead.

I don't think anything of it until it rings again. The same thing happens two more times within the next ten minutes. Finally, I answer with, "Look, either say something or quit fucking call—"

"Tanner?" A female voice comes through the speaker.

"Erin?" I ask, hoping to God that it's her.

"Sorry, I kept hanging up. Just trying to gather my nerves, I guess."

"It's alright. Don't worry about it. Are you okay?"

She gives an enthusiastic, "Yeah, I'm fine. I just wanted to talk to you. I was thinking that maybe I was a little too hasty the other day."

"Oh?"

"Yeah. I mean, I still have no idea what I'm doing, but maybe we could talk some more. And maybe I could see you next time you're back in town."

The smile on my face is one of a man who just hit the lottery.

"I would love that."

She exhales a heavy sigh of relief. "Okay, good. I was worried that you were already hanging out with someone new."

"Nope. Just me."

We are silent for a moment before I say, "So, tell me about your day, beautiful."

Chapter Seventeen

ERIN

A few days have gone by since I decided to reach out and call Tanner. Part of me still has no idea how I'm going to make this whole thing work. My Tanner world and my motherhood world seem like two totally different things, and I am clueless on how to meld the two.

But the other part of me?

That part feels like a teenage girl again, smitten with her new boyfriend. The man can turn my whole day around with one, "Hope you're having a good day, beautiful," text message.

It's a whole different feeling than the sense of dread I would get when Judd would text me. All he would ever text about was when he wanted to complain about something.

Even just thinking about Tanner puts a dopey grin on my face. I haven't felt this giddy in years.

We text throughout the day off and on when either of us has the time, and after the kids go to bed at night, I call him. We don't talk about anything too major—just mainly talk about our days and getting to know each other a little better.

It may not sound like much, but I look forward to it every single evening.

I'm a little surprised that we haven't gotten around to talking about much of the dirty stuff. I'm sure that Tanner is trying to be respectful, but remember that horny feeling that I was having? Talking to him again has only made it worse.

And I still have almost a whole week until he's back in town.

How ever will I pass the time?

Oh yeah, I have three kids with three very busy schedules.

Tonight, we are at my dad's house for a cookout. On the weekends, I have the kids, we try to always see my father—even if it's just for a little while. He lives alone, and I worry about him getting lonely. His grandsons are his world and seeing them always puts a smile on his face.

I watch my kids run around the back yard, playing their own version of football while my dad mans the grill. When I was growing up, my father always made sure my brother and I were taken care of. He made sure we were well-fed and had nice clothes to wear to school, all while doing his best to spend as much time with us as he could. He never acted like we were any type of burden, but it was clear how stressed he always was. He never got to spend much time just being a fun dad, so I really love watching him get to be the best grandpa my boys could ask for.

He piles meat onto the grill, always careful to buy each boy their favorite. One gets chicken wings, one gets steak, and one gets porkchops. I always assure him that they will eat whatever, but he insists that at grandpa's house, they get their choice of what they want to eat.

My phone vibrates on the picnic table in front of me. When I pick it up, I see that it's a text from Tanner. I don't even have to look at it before the smile overtakes my lips. I try to hide it, though, as to not attract attention to myself.

Tanner: Hey babygirl.

I'm loving the new nickname.

I've got a couple more hours of work today, but I wanted to let you know I was thinking about you. Can't wait to talk to you tonight.

Apparently, the smile is back because my dad says, "Alright, who's the guy?"

"Huh?" I look up at him.

"Every time you smile like that, I know you're talking to a guy."

"I don't know what you're talking about," I lie. "I'm watching cute puppy videos. Puppies make me smile like this."

"Erin Mae, I have known you thirty-three years now. I know the difference between your cute puppy face and cute boy face. Are you seeing someone?"

Looking down at my hands, I pick at my non-existent fingernails. "Would that be bad if I was?"

He sits down at the table across from me, running his hand over his scruffy beard. "Not at all. I think it would be great for you to start dating again."

"Really?" I ask, my shock apparent. "Why?"

"Because being a parent shouldn't consume your life. I watch you break your back every single day for those kids, and I love that you're such a great momma. But a long time ago, I watched a man come along, and over the years, I saw him slowly take bits and pieces from you. And while I am under no delusions that you *need* a man, I think it's nice to see you smiling again."

"You never dated," I tell him.

"Oh, darlin', please tell me that you are not using me as the model for your love life," he says with a chuckle.

"Why not? You always made sure we were taken care of."

"You're right. But I was so bitter over the shit that your momma pulled that I completely closed the door on any type of relationship for a long time. It wasn't exactly healthy because I carried that resentment around for a long time. Made for a lot of wasted time."

I'm not sure I want to know the answer to my next question, but I ask it anyway. "Have you dated at all?"

He looks almost as uncomfortable answering the question as I was asking it. "I've dated a little the past few years. Nothing too serious. But I've had some lady friends."

I don't know what exactly that means. And I don't want to.

Letting out a deep sigh, I say, "I'm not sure how to do all this."

"It's kind of like riding a bike."

Both of us realize the awkward inuendo of that statement and both make a face before starting to laugh.

I say, "The whole thing is pretty new. The kids don't know anything about it, and I think I'd like to keep it that way for a while."

"Fair enough." He nods. "What seems to be the problem?"

"The guy seems dang near perfect. I'm just waiting for the other shoe to drop."

"Erin, no man is perfect. We all are a handful in our own right, but if one of them treats you right and tries his hardest to make you happy, I think that's worth something."

There's a sadness in his eyes. He tried so hard to make my momma happy before she ran off. Truth is that I don't think she would've ever been happy here in Maple Oaks. Despite my dad treating her like a queen, she yearned for the bright lights of the big city. Not even her two kids were enough to keep her around.

Putting my hand on top of his, I say, "You know, Momma leaving wasn't your fault. We never blamed you for that."

"I know, kiddo. It took me a long time to realize that she had a lot of issues that no one would be able to fix aside from herself. If I would have figured that out sooner, I may have been more open to the idea of dating—not that I had a lot of time back then."

"That's sort of the problem I'm running into. My schedule is so filled with kid stuff all the time that I am not quite sure how to fit someone else into it."

"Oh, you have every other weekend off, and you know I'm here to be a babysitter whenever you need me. You want to go out on a date when you have the boys, just call me."

"I feel bad doing that," I confess. "It seems like I am out having fun while someone else takes care of my responsibilities."

"First of all, I love any time I get to spend with those kids. The more, the better. And I know what it's like raising your kids without any type of support system. I'll be damned if I'm going to let you go through that same thing. It takes a village, and I'll be more than happy to be your village any day of the week—even if it's just because you need a night off."

"Thanks, Dad."

He gives me a small wink before heading back to the grill to flip the meat. I may have gotten stuck with a shit mother, but my dad more than makes up for it.

And he seems to think me dating again is a good idea. Between him and my friends, they're making it hard to come up with new reasons why this whole thing is a bad idea.

Unlocking my phone, I pull up the message from Tanner once again, ready to respond to it.

But instead, I opt for something a little naughtier. I walk inside the house to bathroom that used to be mine. Now, it's just a guest one that never gets used. After locking the door behind me, I look in the mirror and try to make myself look halfway presentable. I pull my hair down out of its bun and run my fingers through it to fluff it up a little. I can't decide if I look sexy or just plain crazy.

Oh well. Either way, I'm going with it.

I then undo the buttons on my flannel shirt, exposing my bra underneath. It's not one of my cutest ones, but it's also not one of the rattiest either.

The next five minutes are spent with me trying to perfectly adjust *the girls* to pull them from the top of the bra and make them look decent. Then, I take about thirty photos of myself, hoping that just one of them looks good.

When I settle on one that I don't hate, I type:

I miss you too. Maybe our talk tonight will be a little more interesting.

Taking a deep breath, I gather up all my courage before hitting SEND. I put down my phone as I button my shirt back up. Before I can even finish, it rings.

"Hello?" I answer in a low voice.

"Babygirl, are you trying to make my dick hard for the rest of the day?"

"Maybe," I say as I feel my cheeks blush. "Did it work?"

"Fuck yes, it did. I'm going to be sneaking peaks at that picture all day long."

Hearing him say he likes it gets me all tingly inside. "Maybe tonight, you can return the favor."

"Oh, I'm going to do more than that, beautiful."

I'm not sure what that means, but it gets me excited. "Well, you better get back to work so that you can finish on time."

His laugh fills the other end of the phone. "Okay, babygirl. Miss you. Call me tonight."

"Miss you too," I say before hanging up.

Okay, who am I? I'm taking sexy pictures in the guest bathroom of my dad's house and sending them to a boy. Like a dang teenager.

Oh, who am I kidding? I didn't do anything like this when I was a teenager. I was much more of a good girl back then.

I guess it's time for a rebellious streak. Thirty-three isn't too old for that, right?

"Momma, can we read another one?" Joey asks.

"Sweetheart, this was number five. That's your limit for the night."

"But I'm not tired." He draws out the last word so long that he lets out a yawn at the end of it.

"You sure about that?"

"Mmm-hmm," he replies, rubbing his sleepy eyes.

"We will read more tomorrow, I promise," I tell him with a kiss on his forehead. "Now, lay down, so I can tuck you in like a little burrito."

He huffs a little, but he's so tired that it doesn't take much convincing. Spending the evening at my dad's wore all the kids out. The big two passed out before Joey since Joey insists that we read a stack of books every single night.

I run my fingers through his hair a couple times, and he's already about to pass out. I don't know why he fights sleep so hard. When I get the chance to go to bed early, it's amazing.

But then again, I'm not a three-year-old with the fear of missing out on something.

As quietly as I can, I sneak out of his room and go to check on the bigger two before going to my own room. Every night when the three of them are in bed, I let out a huge sigh of relief. Being a mom means I am constantly worrying about them.

Are they safe? Are they fed? Are they warm?

They aren't with me 24/7, and when they're not, those thoughts run through my head constantly—along with a million others. But when I've tucked them into bed, and they are fast asleep having sweet dreams, I feel a sense of calm. On the weekends, they're with Judd, I don't sleep nearly as well because I don't have them ten feet away where I can go check on them anytime I want.

Now that the kids are asleep, I can go take my shower and get ready to enjoy the rest of my evening. I picked up the house earlier while the kids put together a LEGO set so that tonight, I could give Tanner my full attention as soon as possible.

Twenty minutes later, I'm showered, moisturized, and in bed. After I'm comfortable, I dial Tanner's number.

It takes about four rings before he gives a sleepy, "Hello?"

"Oh, no. Did I wake you up?"

"Nope," he says. "I was just resting my eyes."

"I'm so sorry. I wanted to call sooner, but I got shanghaied into reading Joey a handful of books."

"No worries, babygirl."

I can still hear how tired he sounds.

"You must be exhausted," I tell him. "I'll just let you go to bed."

"Whoa, whoa, whoa. Hold up there, beautiful. I've been waiting all damn day to talk to you. I can sleep when I'm dead."

"Are you sure?"

"Absolutely. After your picture earlier, I've barely been able to contain myself all day."

"Did you like it?" I ask.

"Are you kidding? Your tits are a fucking work of art. I could stare at them all day. Hell, I did stare at them all day."

I giggle. "Good."

"Every time I think about it, my cock gets hard all over again."

Feeling naughty, I ask, "Why didn't you send me a picture in return?"

"I didn't know if you'd be into a dick pic," he replies.

"Maybe I would."

"Oh yeah?" He asks. "I can do you one better."

Before I can ask what he means, my phone vibrates against my cheek. When I look at it, I see that's he's requesting to video chat with me. I put in my earbuds before hitting the ACCEPT button so that there's no chance of my kids hearing some strange man in here with me.

Tanner's face pops up on the screen. And it's just as gorgeous as I remember. He gives me a big smile and a, "Hey there, beautiful."

"Hi," I say, smiling back.

"Is this what you wanted to see?" He asks, moving the camera down to his waist.

Much to my surprise, his dick is already out, and holy moly, he has the piercing back in. Immediately, my clit throbs at the thought of him moving inside me with that thing.

"You're sexy," I tell him.

"This is what you do to me," he says. "Just thinking about your tits and your ass or how your pussy feels wrapped around my cock makes me instantly hard."

Okay, the man is taking my horniness to new heights.

"Have you... you know?" I ask.

"Have I what? Have I jerked it, thinking about all the dirty things I want to do to you?"

I swallow the lump in my throat. "Mm-hmm."

"Fuck, yes, I have. I stroke it, imagining I'm fucking into you."

I shift on the bed, trying to lessen the ache between my thighs. Spoiler alert: it doesn't work.

He then asks, "Have you touched yourself while thinking about me?"

The question catches me a little off-guard. Yes, I've thought about him. A lot. I have barely even read my books for inspiration. Thoughts of Tanner have been more than enough to cross the finish line. But I'm not sure I want to say that.

What if he doesn't like it?

But then, it occurs to me that he probably wouldn't have asked if he wasn't going to like it.

"Yes," I say in a meek voice.

"What have you been thinking about?"

"You. Going down on me."

Without giving me time to question my response, he says, "I can't wait until I get to eat your pussy again."

"What else do you want to do to me?"

"Everything that you will let me," he says. "Anything you want me to do or anything you want to try?"

I think for a second. "Honestly, I really haven't tried all that much. My life up until you has been pretty vanilla."

"But the stuff you read about isn't vanilla," he retorts.

I giggle. "No, it's definitely not."

"So, is there anything from your books that you want to try?"

"There is a lot that I wouldn't mind trying," I reply honestly. "I feel like I read about this stuff, but I don't know really what it feels like. Sometimes, it's hard for me to imagine."

"We can try anything you want, beautiful. I'll explore anything you want."

Man, that's equal parts sexy as sin and sweet as sugar.

"You're getting me all turned on," I tell him.

"Show me."

"Come again?"

"Set your phone up, open your legs, and let me see you touch that pretty pussy."

I've never done anything like this, but I do as he asks without thinking twice about it because if I don't find some release soon, I might just explode.

I use a couple of extra pillows to position my phone up so that Tanner can see. Then, I slip out of my panties and toss them onto the floor.

Looking at myself in the phone camera, I don't think this is the most flattering angle. Tanner must like it, though, because he says, "Holy shit, babygirl. I need to be inside that pussy again."

I use two fingers to spread myself open, showing off even more.

"Touch it," he says. "Rub your clit."

My fingers tremble as they move to follow his directions. My heart is about to beat right out of my chest. I let out a moan as I apply pressure to the sensitive area.

When my eyes drift back to the phone, I see that Tanner's done the same thing with his phone, and he's got his dick in his hand, slowly stroking it up and down. The guy just walks around all day with a literal anaconda between his legs.

"I wish I was there, babygirl," he tells me.

"What would you do if you were here?"

"Make that pussy come in every way I could think of. With my tongue. My fingers. My cock." He watches me for a moment before saying, "That's it, beautiful. Play with that clit. Rub it a little faster for me."

I do, and it feels so good. Already my legs are starting to shake. This man isn't even here and is still going to make me come like a faucet.

"Does that feel good, babygirl?"

"Mmm-hmm."

"Slide one finger inside and tell me how wet you are."

With my other hand, I take my middle finger and push it inside. "I'm so wet," I moan.

"Put your finger in your mouth. Lick it off and tell me how good it tastes."

I do as he commands, putting on a show as I lick the tangy liquid off.

He lets out a low groan. "Holy fuck, that's so hot. I'm so fucking hard."

Oh yeah. I can see that.

"Keep rubbing your clit," he tells me. "I want to watch you come."

My eyes stay fixed on Tanner stroking himself as I bring myself closer to the edge. Half an hour ago, just the thought of this would make me blush. I probably would have said I would have never done it because I would be too self-conscious.

But here I am.

Spread eagle on the bed and touching myself for my boyfriend.

Is he my boyfriend?

Geez, at this point, I would sure hope so.

I'm getting close. It feels amazing, but I try to keep myself quiet so that I don't wake up anyone. When I start to come, I have to bite into the side of my hand to muffle myself. My eyes squeeze shut as my pussy contracts.

I open my eyes just in time to see Tanner letting out his own release. He continues to stroke as he shoots his load everywhere. A little drop hangs from his piercing, and I wish I was there to lick it off.

"Lord, Erin... you are so fucking sexy."

I will never get tired of hearing him say that.

When we have both cleaned ourselves up, I figure that he will be ready to get off the phone, but he surprises me when he says, "Alright, babygirl. Tell me all about your day."

A sexy man I just had hot phone sex with now actually wants to hear about my day? If I didn't know any better, I'd swear I hit the jackpot.

Chapter Eighteen

TANNER

"Come on, boys. Time to haul ass. I want this job done tonight so that we can head home in the morning," I tell my team.

Although we've been working hard to get this done, we ran into a few snafus along the way. Now, it's time to kick it into high gear because I'm not getting home late. No way in hell am I missing any time with Erin.

"What's your hurry?" Harry asks.

Of course, he would be the one to ask. Harry is in his forties and can't stand his wife. I swear if he could stay traveling 365 days of the year so that he would never have to go home. Sometimes, he moves so slow it's like he's got concrete in his boots. I'd love to replace him with someone else, but that decision is up to someone with a bigger paycheck than me.

"Well, Harry, most of us have people at home that we *want* to get home to," I tell him.

He scoffs. "Oh, bullshit. You don't have anyone."

Oh, bud. If only you knew.

When I'm at work, I tend to keep my personal life private. I'm not one to kiss and tell or brag about my conquests. I'm certainly not about to brag about anything that Erin and I do. In fact, I haven't talked about Erin at all. I'd love to brag about her all day long, but I think I'm too scared to jinx it.

"Even if I don't, I'd rather be home than here with you crazy bastards. I'd like to sleep in my own bed tomorrow night if you don't mind."

Or in Erin's.

Harry drags ass but still manages to get back to work. At this point, I don't care if I have to finish this entire job by myself as long as it gets me home sooner.

Our evening chats have been cut a little short because her youngest son, Joey, has been having bad dreams and climbing into bed with her. Although we still talk a little and then text all day, it's not enough. I need to see her. I need to have her in my arms.

The other night, I was floored when she sent me the sexy photo. And even more shocked when she touched herself over video chat. The woman has no idea how sexy she is, but I sure as shit do. I have not been able to stop thinking about it ever since. I was hoping for a replay, but her son in her bed doesn't accommodate that.

It's alright. I'll just have to make up for lost time this weekend.

Lying on the bed in my hotel room, I flip through channels. We managed to finish everything up today. As tempted as I was to just go ahead and drive home, I didn't think it was a good idea with how exhausted I am. I don't need to be falling asleep at the wheel.

Plus, it's not like I'm able to see Erin until tomorrow evening anyway. I figure when I get back to my place, I will try to get a few things done before I meet up with her. I want zero distractions during our time together.

My phone vibrates next to me. Looking at it, I mumble, "Speak of the devil."

I answer with a, "Hey, babygirl. How are you doing?"

"Okay, I guess," she says. "Tired. Joey in my bed every night isn't making it easy to get much sleep. I never knew such a tiny human being could take up so much space. I swear all night, I had feet in my face."

"Sounds rough."

"I know they say that one day, I will miss these days. And I'm sure I will. But right now, I'd like to just get a little bit of sleep." She laughs.

"You can get lots of sleep this weekend," I tell her.

"Something tells me neither one of us will be getting much sleep this weekend."

A smile tugs at my lips. "Oh yeah?"

"I think you and I have some *very* fun activities that will keep us wide awake."

Aaaaand my dick's hard again.

As much as I'm looking forward to getting her naked and doing every dirty thing I can think of, I also don't want her to think that stuff is all I care about. Because as wonderful as it is, I don't want that to be the only thing our relationship is built on. I've played that game before, and I want what I have with Erin to be more than that.

"Hey," I begin. "Let me take you out tomorrow night."

"What do you mean? Is that some kind of inuendo?"

I laugh. "No, I mean let me take you out on a date. A *real* date."

She seems surprised but pleasantly so. "Okay. A date sounds nice. What do you have in mind?"

"It's a surprise," I tell her. Truthfully, I have no idea what we're going to do, so I guess it's kind of a surprise to both of us. I'm sure I'll think of something good, though.

"What should I wear? Do I need to dress up?"

"Up to you. I want you to be comfortable."

"Hmm. Okay, I think I can find something." She pauses a moment before asking, "So, how was your day?"

Despite all of the things that she and I do or talk about, hearing her ask me that every night is the highlight for me. No one has ever asked me that before and really cared about the answer. It makes me feel all warm and fuzzy hearing the woman that I'm crazy about ask me.

Chapter Nineteen

Erin

"You look nice," Chris tells me as I come walking down the stairs. "You hanging out with Aunt Gina and Aunt Nancy again tonight?"

"Uh, yeah," I fib, not ready to divulge the fact that I have a date.

"Boys!" I call to all of them. "Make sure you have all of your stuff. Your dad is going to flip his lid if he needs to come back here three weekends in a row!"

He'd probably think that I did it on purpose just to be spiteful. Little does he know that the less I have to interact with him, the happier I will be.

A knock on the door gets Charlie to let out a single bark before going and hiding behind the couch. I'm pretty sure he knows the sound of Judd's loud truck and ducks for cover. I can't say I blame him. I want to do the same.

I open the door, and Judd looks me up and down. "You're awfully dressed up."

"Thanks," I say, not sure how to respond.

"Wasn't a compliment."

How on Earth did I stay married to this man as long as I did?

"Oh, I wanted to talk to you," I begin as he sighs and rolls his eyes. "Chris needs to study for his math test on Monday. His grade is slipping, and if he fails this test, he will be suspended from all sports."

"Why did you let his grade get so low?"

How is this my fault?

"Uh," I stammer.

"Look, I'm not having him spend all of his weekend studying."

"Judd, I'm not saying he needs to study all—"

"It's MY weekend. I'm not wasting my time with him doing that shit. You should have had him studying all week. Maybe you can spend your time finding him a tutor."

Before I have a chance to respond, he says, "I'll wait for them in the truck. Tell them to hurry up."

Why couldn't he have just waited in the truck the whole time?

The boys all come thundering back down the stairs a moment later and give me a quick hug before they walk out the door.

The moment I close it behind them, I can feel my blood pressure skyrocketing. So much for cooperation between parents. How hard is it to have Chris look over his study guide for an hour? But of course, I always have to be the bad guy. If Chris gets kicked off the football team, it will be my fault that I didn't make him study enough. It will be my fault that I didn't hire a tutor. But then, Chris goes to his dad's, and it's all fun and games all weekend long.

I know the kids love their dad. And by most accounts, Judd is a decent one. But I'm not sure I can continue on with all of this crap for the rest of my life especially if he keeps treating me like I'm beneath him instead of his equal.

And the worst part is that I let him do it. When he's around, I turn into a metaphorical punching bag. I may as well lay down and let him use me as a doormat. I spent so many years trying not to make waves, and it's hard to get out of that habit.

I take a few deep breaths and try to push any thoughts of Judd out of my head. Tanner will be here any minute. I've been so excited about this night, and I'm not going to let Judd ruin it.

Lord knows the man has already ruined enough in my life.

I take a few deep breaths and put on my sandals as I wait for Tanner to show up. I had no clue what to wear, so I decided on a sun dress with a sweater because yes, it's hot as heck in Texas, but I still get cold when I'm inside buildings that have the air conditioning blasting.

Another knock at the door.

But this time, excitement washes over me instead of dread.

As I open it, Tanner stands leaning against one side of the doorway with his hands in his pockets. How is it that he's gotten even more attractive?

"Hey, beautiful," he says with a wide smile.

"I missed you," I blurt.

As he takes a step toward me, he whispers, "You have no fucking idea."

Before I know it, his mouth is on mine as one hand tangles in my hair while the other wraps around my waist to pull me closer. It's fiercely passionate, and it takes no time at all before we get lost in the moment.

When he pulls back, I let out a disappointed moan.

He says, "As much as I want to continue this, if we go any further, I'm going to get you naked."

"What's wrong with that?" I say, giving a light kiss to his neck.

"Well, as soon as I get you naked, I don't plan on stopping worshipping your body for several hours, and we're both going to need some food first."

I stick out my bottom lip to pout but give a short, "Okay."

He looks me up and down. "But let me say that you look absolutely stunning."

"You sure? I wasn't sure if it would be proper motorcycle attire. We can take my SUV if you want."

He smiles. "Well, as much as I would love you see you hike up that dress to swing your leg over my bike, I actually also have a truck that I drove tonight."

"You're just full of surprises, aren't you?"

"I have to keep you guessing," he says with a wink.

I grab my purse and check on Charlie before we head out. He helps me into the truck before going around to the other side and climbing in himself.

"Nice truck," I say. It really is. Looks like it can't be very old, and I'm guessing he's done some upgrades to it.

"Thanks. I like it, but I've spent too much money on it."

"Is this what you drive to work?"

He shakes his head back and forth. "They give me a truck to drive, so I don't have to pay for gas or put a ton of miles on my own vehicle. I keep all my tools in it too."

"So, how often do you drive this?"

"Not often enough. I get it to drive when I don't want to drive the motorcycle in bad weather. But here in Texas, there's not a whole lot of that." He laughs. "I really should drive it more."

We make some more small talk as we drive to a restaurant. It's a couple towns over, and I haven't heard of it before, but it looks like a cute little Italian place.

When he parks, he says, "Full disclosure, we aren't actually eating here."

My brow furrows. "What do you mean? What are we doing here?"

"Well, I planned on just getting some takeout and take the food somewhere a little more intimate."

I have no idea what he has in mind, but he has me sold with the word 'intimate'. He pulls up the menu on his phone and has me pick out what I want. I settle on the chicken alfredo since I'm sure that I will get anything with red sauce all over my dress because... well, that's just who I am as a person.

Half an hour later, we are pulling into the drive-in movie theatre.

"The drive-in?" I ask. "Man, I haven't been here in years."

"You haven't taken your kids?"

"Three kids shoved in a car, pumped full of sugar? That doesn't sound like the best idea."

We both start laughing.

"You need a truck," he says. "Then, you can shove them all in the bed to watch. You can sit back there with them or sit in the cab where it's quiet."

"You make some good points." I smile. "So, what are we going to watch?"

"You pick."

While we are in line, I look at the list of movies that's on the old sign at the entrance. "I'm not sure that I'm the best person to pick. I don't think I've heard of any of these."

"Even better. Just pick what sounds good based on the title. Nothing else known about it."

"Oh, geez. That sounds even worse than judging a book based on the cover." Looking a moment more, I pick one that sounds like it will be some type of action movie. Good enough, I guess.

He backs into a parking spot not too close but not too far from the screen. "One second," he tells me.

He jumps out and grabs a few things from the backseat. He's so quick I don't even see what he grabs. A few minutes later, he opens my door for me and leads me around to the bed of the truck. He's completely transformed it with blankets and pillows, making it the perfect place to watch an outdoor movie.

He even has a small little step stool to help me climb up into it. He's really thought of everything.

He holds my hand while I step up and kick off my sandals to get comfortable. Before he joins me, he gets the plastic containers out of the bag from the restaurant and hands one of them to me. When he sits down, he opens another bag and pulls out a bottle of wine and two plastic cups.

"Sorry, I don't have any real wine glasses," he says.

"Hey, I'm surprised you've thought of this much. I would have been okay with some McDonalds."

He laughs. "You're an easy woman to please, huh?"

"I have my moments." I take a bite of my pasta, and it's delicious. "Holy cow. This is amazing. Why have I never heard of this place before?"

"Most people outside of their town haven't heard of it. They don't do any kind of advertising because the owners want to keep the place small. It's a husband and wife who opened it over forty years ago. They've poured their hearts and souls into the place the whole time. You can tell they really love it."

"Man, I wish I was that passionate about something... anything." I'm a little surprised by my sudden confession. That's something I never thought I would say out loud, let alone to another person.

"There's still time, you know—to find your passion. You've got a whole lot of living left to do."

My phone vibrates, and I check it just to make sure it isn't anything having to do with one of the kids.

"Everything okay?" Tanner asks.

"Yeah, it's just my dad. I showed him how to send memes, and now, he sends me a few a day."

"It's good that you and him are so close. Have you heard from your brother lately?"

I'm surprised he remembers me talking about Wes. I just brought him randomly one day.

"No, but my dad has. I guess he's dating someone—not that he tells anyone any type of details about his life."

"Maybe he just hasn't met anyone he really cares about."

"What do you mean?" I ask.

"I told my brother about you. Couldn't wait to tell him. I would have told the other one, but I haven't talked to him."

I can't hide the smile on my face. "So, what you're saying is that you really care about me?"

His blue eyes look into mine. "Hell, yes, I do."

Looking back down at my phone, I say softly, "Back at you."

He leans in and gives me a soft kiss on the cheek.

Soon enough, we finish eating and the movie starts. There aren't a whole lot of cars parked in front of this screen, and once we are a few minutes in, I can see why. The movie is awful. So awful that we are both hysterically laughing at how absurd it is.

Think Jackass in outer space.

"Next time," I tell him. "Don't let me pick the movie."

"Eh, I don't care what we watch as long as we do it together."

He motions for me to sit between his legs, and he rubs my shoulders and plays with my hair. It feels great, but I am feeling a little more frisky. My fingers trail up his thighs—back and forth, each time getting a little bit closer to his dick.

I let out a shiver as he whispers in my ear, "Are you wanting something?"

"Maybe."

"Right here? What if someone sees?"

My shoulders shrug. "Let them watch."

He lets out a frustrated grunt. "You have to stop saying things like that, or you're going to make my cock explode without even touching it."

He grabs one of the thicker blankets and makes sure my bottom half is completely covered from prying eyes. With the walls of the truck bed, though, I doubt that anyone could see much anyway unless they were actually poking their head in.

He hikes up my dress and slides my panties down my legs before pulling my thighs apart.

His fingers lightly rub along each of my lower lips. "Do you know how much I've missed this pussy?" He asks.

"It's missed you too."

His fingers slowly start to play with my clit, giving it light touches to start with before applying more pressure.

Whispering in my ear again, he asks, "Do you think you'll be able to be quiet? I don't want anyone else hearing the noises I'll have you making."

"I'll try," I giggle.

He pulls the blanket up further so that his other hand can slip under my dress and tease my nipples.

"Does this turn you on, babygirl? The idea that anyone could see us right now."

I frantically nod because I can't believe how much this excites me. It's a scene right out of one of my books.

He continues to play with my clit while the other hand leaves my breasts and moves lower. He takes two fingers and slides them inside me. He curls them and starts moving in an upward motion. I don't know what kind of sorcery he is doing, but it feels amazing. Almost more than I can take.

Keeping quiet is practically torture because all I want to do right now is scream Tanner's name. I'm glad the movie is loud because it's at least halfway hiding my heavy breathing—not to mention that my vagina is so wet that Tanner fingering me is making all kinds of noise.

"Do you want to come?" He asks.

I nod.

"Do you think you can keep quiet?"

Another nod.

But his fingers stop all their movements. I let out the most pathetic moan you've ever heard.

"I don't think you can," he says.

"I can. I promise," I plead.

"Are you sure?" He draws out the last word.

"Positive!"

With that, he goes back to work. I do my best to stay quiet, but it's so hard. Tanner seems to be an expert on making me come, but somehow, this feels different. Feels more intense than anything I've felt before.

He keeps me right on the edge until there's another loud part in the movie. When the action starts blaring again, he uses his fingers to rub my clit faster and harder. Just when I'm about to fly over the edge, his other hand covers my mouth to muffle my inevitable scream.

I come so hard that my pussy squirts everywhere. I didn't even think it was possible for me to do that, but Tanner swooped in to prove me wrong yet again. There's a whole new level of hotness added by the idea that anyone could walk by at any time and see what we are doing. I try to stay still as to not draw attention to myself, but do you know how hard that is when your vagina has basically been turned into a water hose?

As my body starts to still, Tanner leans in once again—this time, to whisper, "Good girl."

How is it that I've barely known this man long at all, yet he commands my body like he's been doing it for years?

My chest heaves as I struggle to catch my breath. My eyes try to focus on what's going on in the movie, but I don't know, and honestly, I don't care.

There is only one thing I can think about right now.

Turning back to look at him, I say, "Take me home, baby."

Chapter Twenty

TANNER

"Take them off," Erin tells me, pointing to my pants.

We barely made it through the door before we were all over each other. Making her come at the drive-in was so hot I almost made a mess in my jeans, so when she told me to bring her home, I didn't hesitate.

I try leading her upstairs, but she detours to the couch instead. Whatever works. As long as I get to fuck her, I don't care where we do it.

I take off my jeans and get ready to grab the condom out of my wallet, but she stops me. Instead, she sinks to her knees and angles my cock to her mouth. She may not know it, but Erin is a fucking sex kitten.

She takes a minute to look at my piercing while she slowly strokes me.

With a wicked little grin, she says, "It's even sexier in person."

"Just wait until I fuck you with it."

Another little grin before she sucks the head into her mouth. Her pretty eyes look up at me as she uses her tongue to play with the metal.

"Fuck, Erin," I hiss through my teeth. "That feels so fucking good."

She takes me as far as she can until the piercing hits the back of her throat. She moves slowly, determined to wring every ounce of pleasure from me that she can.

Her fingers tickle my balls, and I have to fist my hand in her hair for some type of stability. I continue to let her set the pace, though. I refuse to give her more than she can handle.

It feels amazing, but I need to be inside her. There's no way I'm not getting her off again tonight.

I gently pull her to her feet before turning her around and hiking up her dress. After we got done at the drive-in, I told her to keep the panties off. I'm glad I did because seeing her pussy peek out as she bends over is the definition of perfection.

I get the condom and roll it on as fast as I can, still careful not to let it get snagged on the piercing. I push into her, slowly, giving her time to get used to it. But she doesn't seem to need it. She moves her ass, pushing back into me, urging me to go harder and faster.

Good lord, this woman is perfect.

She's everything.

"Do you know much I just love laying here with you?" Erin asks as we lie in bed together.

"Well, it's definitely a highlight for me too," I tell her. Her head lies on my chest as I run my fingers through her hair.

She looks up at me. "I'm serious. I never thought I would have this again, and... I don't know..."

Her eyes move away, but I say, "Hey, talk to me. You can tell me anything."

Her voice cracks as she starts to speak again. "It just makes me feel like I can be happy again. I mean, I still don't know how this part of my life with you fits into my life with kids, but I can't help but feel like maybe happiness really is possible again."

"Babygirl, I can tell you right now that I will do anything in my power to make this work, and I would move heaven and hell to make you happy."

I feel like I've been waiting for Erin to walk into my life, and there's no way in hell I will let her go without a fight. I tried once, and just look at how that turned out. I was miserable without her.

There's no doubt in my mind that I am falling in love with this woman. I'm not going to say that, though, because I know she still has concerns. Instead, I will try to squash those doubts until I know she feels comfortable.

Right now, the schedule we are on works because of our circumstances—her kids and my job. But one day, I'm going to want to wake up with her every single morning just like this. I'm not going to want to go without her for two weeks at a time.

Giving her a kiss on the top of her head, I ask, "Why don't we go downstairs, and I'll cook us some pancakes?"

"Let me get this straight—you want to give me orgasms *and* make me pancakes?"

"And I'll even rub your back and call you pretty."

"Dang. I'd like to see my vibrator do that."

We both get up and head downstairs to the kitchen. I have to ask where a few things are, but then, I insist that I have it under control, and Erin doesn't need to help.

"Are you sure?" She asks. "I'm not really used to doing *nothing* while other people do things for me."

"Well, you better get used to it, babygirl. Because there's going to be a whole lot more of it happening."

I watch her walk over to the refrigerator and pull out a jar of pickles. She unscrews the lid and grabs one of the spears before putting the jar back.

"You realize I'm making pancakes, right?" I ask.

"Yeah. So?"

"It's like eight AM."

"There's never a bad time for pickles."

"Pickles and pancakes. What a combination." I laugh.

"What can I say? I'm a pickle gal."

"Sounds dirty."

"Can I be *your* pickle gal? I'll tickle your pickle."
She does a cute little dance that has me cracking
up.

"I would love it if you would tickle my pickle."
Could she be any cuter?

As she's dancing, she swings her arm too hard
and smacks her fingers on the counter. Her
face scrunches up as she cries, "Ouch! Mother
fluffernutter. Son of a gun."

I walk over to her and raise her hand to my lips
and kiss the sore fingers. "You know for someone
with such a filthy mouth in bed, you sure do censor
yourself any other time."

She smiles. "When the boys were little, I really
tried to watch it because they were little parrots
who would repeat everything I said. I just got used
to making a G-rated version of everything. Plus,
Judd thought it wasn't *ladylike*."

"Even in the bedroom?"

"*Everywhere.* Not that he ever made it good
enough to warrant any type of dirty talk."

Erin implying that I make it good enough to talk
like a sailor makes me puff out my chest with pride.

When I finish the pancakes, we sit down on the
couch to eat.

There's something I want to ask. I feel like I'm
looking a gift horse in the mouth, but I have to ask
it anyway.

"Hey, Erin?"

"Yeah?" She says, taking a bite. "Mmm. This is
good."

"Thanks. I have to ask—what made you call me? I'm not going to lie when I left here, I didn't think you were going to give me a second thought."

"If I say I just missed you, would you believe me?" She gives a nervous smile.

"If that's your story, and you're sticking to it." I laugh.

She takes a deep breath. "Truth is I figured out that Judd already had a woman living with him. He brought her to Alex's soccer game."

"Oh."

"Wow, that makes me sound like I'm doing this as just a way to get back at him or something."

"No—"

She cuts me off. "That's not it. I couldn't stop thinking about you, but there was a voice in my head telling me that Judd and I had a deal to try to do what was best for our kids. Seeing him with her made me realize that he doesn't care about any of that. I've been so busy trying to keep the peace for someone who wouldn't do the same for me."

Sometimes, I don't know whether to want to punch this man or thank him.

I want to punch him for all the emotional damage that he's done to Erin over the years. I can tell that he's gotten under her skin in the worst way possible—and treated her like shit.

I want to thank him because I get to be the one to make it right and show her that not all men are the same.

She grabs me by the chin and angles me so that I'm looking at her. "I don't want you to think that

I'm doing this for any other reason than that I want to be with you."

"Glad to hear it, beautiful."

Chapter Twenty-one

"Okay, I'll let you pick what we watch," I tell Tanner. "But it has to be something more interesting than Lord of the Rings. Last time, that put me right to sleep."

He looks at me. "And I can forgive you for that... once. Next time, I'll spank that sexy ass of yours."

"Maybe we *should* try to watch Lord of the Rings again," I joke.

"Oh, no. This time, we are watching something more interesting to keep you awake."

I give a small pout, but he doesn't notice. After our sex last night with Tanner's piercing, I can't seem to get enough. It was incredible. It touched places I didn't even know I had.

"You underestimate my ability to fall asleep anytime, anywhere," I tell him. "So, what did you pick?"

"Game of Thrones. Ever heard of it?"

I roll my eyes. "Just because I don't watch a lot doesn't mean I live under a rock."

"Any idea what it's about?"

I shake my head. "Not a clue."

"Can I ask you something?" Tanner questions after a long pause.

"Sure."

"What did you and Judd do? I know you said you didn't watch a lot of movies and stuff, but from what you say, it doesn't seem like you guys did much together."

"That was random," I tell him. "Truthfully, we didn't spend a lot of time together at all at the end. Typically, we didn't even sleep in the same bed. One of us would crash on the couch. When we first got together, we loved going to the movies, but that gets a lot more expensive when you have three kids to take with you. Between work, driving the kids around, and keeping the house in order, I didn't have time for a lot of other stuff. During hunting season, Judd would go hunting almost every weekend, and I was just happy to have him out of the house."

He grabs my hand. "Erin, I'm really sorry you had to go through all that."

"It's fine," I reply, shaking it off.

With his eyes fixed on mine, he says, "No, it's not. You should have never been in a situation where someone made you feel like that." He slides off the couch and gets on his knees in front of me. "You should be treated like a queen."

I run my finger across his cheek. "You're doing a pretty good job of it so far."

"I'm going to make you a promise."

"You don't have to promise me anything, baby."

He wraps his arms around my waist. "I want to. I promise that you will never have to carry the brunt of anything in this relationship. It's a partnership. Fifty-fifty. That includes housework, cooking, and everything else. And no matter what, we will make time for us. I don't care what I have to do, but we will make it happen."

I love how sweet he is. I know that things aren't always that easy when you add kids into the mix, but it's nice that he's willing to try. Judd never was.

Every moment I spend with Tanner convinces me a little more that this whole thing could work. He convinces me that good men are out there. I've always known my father was a good man, but with the way Judd treated me, I wondered if my dad was a zebra amongst horses.

He joins me back on the couch and turns on Game of Thrones. We watch the entire first episode in silence, and when it's over, Tanner is anxious to hear what I think.

"It was good," I say. "But why are there like a million characters? Seems like it's going to be hard to keep them all straight."

He smiles. "That's what you have me for."

I pinch his cheeks. "Okay, my little nerd."

"This nerd is going to eat your pussy until you can't take anymore later."

"Once again, there you go, threatening me with a good time."

He lets out a deep laugh. "Do you want to watch the next episode?"

He sounds so excited that I just can't tell him no. "Sure. Let me run upstairs real quick and get the boys' laundry to throw in the washer."

"Alright, and I'll make us some popcorn."

I quickly pad up the stairs and head into Chris and Alex's room. Something catches my eye and makes me stop dead in my tracks.

"Son of a—"," I mutter.

An empty snake cage.

As quickly as I can, I run downstairs. "Tanner!" I call and then find him in the kitchen.

"What's wrong?" He asks when he sees the look on my face.

"Tater Tot has sort of... escaped."

He looks confused until he puts two and two together and remembers who Tater Tot is. "Motherfucker!" He sits on the island counter and pulls his knees up to his chest. "You're telling me there is a snake loose in this house?"

"Well, yes. But a very, very tiny snake."

"Size doesn't matter, Erin."

I start laughing so hard I snort. "Oh, it most certainly does."

"This is not the time for jokes," he scolds. "There's a blood-thirsty animal on the loose."

"You're being ridiculous. You know that? Joey even plays with the snake."

"I would rather be ridiculous than dead."

"Okay, well, I'm going to go upstairs and look for the little guy. Chances are, he's still in the boys' room." I can tell that Tanner isn't going to be able to relax until Tater Tot is safely back inside his tank.

"You're going to leave me alone? What if I see him?"

"Do you want to come with me?"

"No. What if he's up there?"

I roll my eyes. "Good grief. Just stay there. I'll try to hurry up. If you want something to keep yourself amused, finish making our popcorn."

I get all the way back upstairs before I hear a loud, high-pitched, "Erin!"

I run back to the kitchen and see Tanner, who is now standing on the counter, holding a frying pan like some sort of weapon.

"What's wrong?"

He points to the cabinet where the popcorn is, and I see Tater Tot slithering between the boxes. "Looks like someone was sniffing for food," I say as I grab the little guy.

He wraps himself around my hand for stability. "See?" I show Tanner. "He's not so bad."

"Tater Tot will haunt my nightmares."

"Okay, I see the dramatic part of the evening is still going strong," I say, walking out of the room to take the snake back upstairs. Once he's safely contained, I make sure the lid is securely on the tank before going to find Tanner again.

He's moved from the kitchen to the couch. His arms are crossed over his chest, and his knees bob up and down.

"Are you okay?" I ask him.

He nods. "Yeah. Sorry. Snakes just freak me the fuck out."

"I can see that. Maybe I can help you calm down a little."

I sink onto my knees in front of him, pushing his thighs open. He's just wearing his boxers since we've spent most of the weekend in bed. I undo the little button and pull his dick out through the front opening.

I take his still-soft member and suck it into my mouth.

"Shit, babygirl," Tanner moans as he begins to harden.

Slowly, I tease his piercing with my tongue before moving him down my throat.

Looking up at Tanner, I see his eyes fixed on exactly what I'm doing. "Fuck, you look so good with that dick in your mouth."

He leans down to pull my tits out of the top of my tank top. "There," he says. "That's the perfect view."

Flattening my tongue, I run it along the big vein on the underside of his dick. I take my time, changing up my movements. Sucking, licking, and stroking. I get him close and then change it up, building up the pleasure inside him.

When he isn't able to sit still anymore, I hollow out my cheeks and suck hard as I take him as far down my throat as I can.

"Holy shit, babygirl. If you don't stop, I'm going to come."

Knowing that's the point, I continue on, doing the exact same thing. He lets out a loud, primal moan as he fills my mouth with his release.

After I swallow every drop, he says, "You're fucking perfect. Do you know that?"

Chapter Twenty-two

TANNER

After I leave Erin so that she can be ready for the kids to come home, I decide that I'm not quite ready to go home myself. So, I stop in to see what my mom's doing.

"Momma, you home!" I call as I walk in the front door of her house. She's remarried now, so I probably should have knocked. Don't want to walk in on something I don't want to see.

Thankfully, she comes walking out of the kitchen. "Hey, darlin'! I didn't even know you were in town!"

Her fiery red hair is pulled back with a claw clip. My mother has looked the same for as long as I can remember. She's always been a pretty woman, which is why she never had trouble finding men to keep her company. As I look at her now, though, I see the laugh lines around her mouth starting to form, and a few of her roots are turning grey.

Honestly, with her putting up with three boys, I'm surprised she didn't have greys much sooner.

She wraps her arms around my back to give me a big hug. It doesn't last long, though, because she pulls back to slap me in the shoulder.

"Why don't you ever tell me when you're home?"

"Sorry, Momma."

"Oh, I guess you're forgiven. Come on in the kitchen. Dinner's almost done."

My eyebrows shoot up. "You cooked?"

She turns to me with her lips pursed. "You know better than that. Rob is cooking."

I throw my hand over my heart. "Thank God."

Another slap.

We get to the kitchen, and Mom's new husband, Rob, stands at the stove. "Hey there, Tanner!" He smiles. "I'm making some vegetable soup if you're hungry."

"Sounds great," I tell him.

Rob seems to be exactly what my mother needs. After forty years of her always finding the wrong men, she finally found a good one. He doesn't have a whole lot of drama or a criminal record, and I'm pretty sure his credit score is even squeaky clean.

It took over half her life, but I think my mother finally got out of her *bad boy* phase.

"So, what have you been up to when you're not working?" She asks, grabbing a Coke out of the fridge and handing it to me.

"I... uh... I actually met someone."

Her eyes go wide. "Ooooh?"

I debated whether or not I was going to say anything to her about Erin, but truth be told, I'm crazy about this woman, and I want to scream it from the rooftops.

"Yeah. Her name is Erin."

"She one of the local college girls?"

I shake my head. "No, actually, she's a little older than me."

She gives me the classic *mother* look. "Tanner James... how much older? You haven't bagged yourself a cougar, have you?"

Rob and I both look at my mother like she's lost her mind. "Mother!" I cry. "No, she's not a cougar. She's only thirty-three."

She uses her fingers to count the years between us before saying, "Oh, that's not that bad."

"What does she do for a living?"

"She works at a dentist office."

"When do we get to meet her?" She croons.

Here's the thing. My mother has never been *this* mother. She always cared about her boys, but she was never all that invested as a mom. She only half paid attention to our grades and always tried to be more of a friend than a mom. Growing up, that had its pros and its cons. Now that we are grown, she tries to fall more into the motherly role.

I don't mind it, I guess, but it's strange. When I was a teenager, and I told her I was dating someone, she would just tell me to wear a condom.

"I don't know," I say. "It's a little complicated."

"Uh-oh. What's wrong with her?"

"Nothing," I defend. "But she has kids."

"Kids? As in plural?"

I nod. "Yeah, three boys."

That motherly look is back, and I'm betting I'm not going to like what she's going to say next. "Now, son, what do you know about dating a woman with three kids?"

"Ha!" I blurt. "Do you not see the irony in that statement? You dated every guy in the world when YOU had three kids. I'm pretty sure you didn't make them fill out a survey on how qualified they were to take on that role."

"Exactly. And I probably should have. I think that I would know a thing or two about this. I dated a whole slew of men who didn't know the first thing about dating a woman with kids."

"And I *watched* you date all those guys. Don't you think that I picked up some tips on how *not* to act?" I feel myself raising my voice, but I try to calm down. No matter how upset I may be getting, I don't think it's appropriate to yell at my mother.

She rubs her fingers along the lines on her forehead. "Tanner, all I'm saying is that it's a big undertaking. And you're on the road ninety percent of the time. Not to mention the fact that you blow through money like it's your job."

"I'm sorry," I interrupt. "Is this some sort of intervention for how awful you think I am?"

"Not at all. I think you're a wonderful man, and I'm so proud of you. I know how much you want to be a husband and a father. I'm just worried that you're trying to skip to the end. Haven't you always wanted kids of your own? Do you think a woman with three already is going to want to have more?"

"I don't know, Momma. We haven't talked about it."

"That's my point. Maybe you shouldn't get serious with this woman until you have had these talks. If she doesn't want to have more kids, are you okay with stepping in and playing daddy to the kids had with someone else?"

"They have a dad," I defend. "He has them every other weekend."

"And if you get with their mother, don't you think that some of that burden will fall on you the other majority of the time that *she* has them? If you think that you won't end up carrying a large part of the weight, you're crazy."

When I don't immediately respond, she tries to put on her best calming voice. "I just feel like maybe you're sick of the dating scene, and you're trying to skip to the happy ending. You want to step into someone else's life, and it just doesn't quite work that way. Wouldn't you rather go on the journey with someone who hasn't done it before?"

My mother has become the queen of hypocrisy, and I think I've heard enough.

Standing up, I say, "If you would have kept quiet for two seconds, you would know that I'm crazy about this woman. I find myself falling in love with her. She could have ten kids, and it wouldn't change that. Thanks for the Coke, but I should be going."

"Tanner," she calls after me.

But all I do is say, "See you later, Rob. Sorry I couldn't stay for dinner."

As I'm walking out of the house, I hear her husband say, "Tammy, what the heck is wrong with you?"

I don't stick around to hear her answer.

Still not ready to go home to my empty apartment, I drive around town aimlessly, thinking about everything my mother said. Don't get me wrong; I think that she's completely out of line. She better get a whole bowl of sugar cubes for that high horse of hers.

But her words keep ringing in my head over and over. I don't mind the fact that Erin has kids. I actually love that about her. It makes her infinitely more complex than any woman I've ever dated. But it's not like she and I have had any type of conversation about what a future may look like.

Of course, we haven't. It's only been a couple of weeks, and I haven't even met her kids yet.

But when I picture a future with this woman, what do I see?

I have no idea.

Since I'm absentmindedly driving, I find myself going past Erin's house. There's a giant pick-up truck in the driveway, and I assume it's Judd. Three boys come flying out of the backseat and go running toward the front door. They all tell their dad bye before going inside.

Is my mother right?

Am I just trying to skip to the good part without going through all the steps to get there?

I may only be twenty-five, but I've dated a lot of women—and slept with even more. Having a mother who wasn't always present when I was younger meant that I was fooling around with girls when I was way too young. I know most thirteen-year-old boys are out there, trying to find a girl to fool around with. Most of them don't do it so young, though.

Maybe that's why I'm so eager to settle down—because I am tired of all of the petty games that come with casually dating/fucking. My life is always in a constant state of flux with as much as I travel. It would be nice to have a constant for me to come home to.

Every time I have tried to tell a woman I'm ready to settle down, they have one of two reactions.

One, they laugh at me as though there's no way I can be serious. They tell me that your twenties are meant for having fun, and they aren't ready to give that up.

Or two, they agree with me in that they want something more serious. But then, they get a taste of my work schedule and tell me that I'm not the one they want to settle down with.

Did all of the pieces just fall into place perfectly with Erin? *Too* perfectly?

A woman who is as done with the dating scene as I am and who is ready to start a life. My mother is right, though. Erin already started a life with someone else. Am I just trying to make myself fit into the hole that Judd left?

My phone chimes through the speakers of my truck, and I look at the screen to see who it is.

Text Message from Erin.

Hitting play, I hear the monotone voice coming through the speakers reading the message, but all I hear is Erin.

"Hey, baby. Just wanted to say how great of a weekend I had with you. I'm already looking forward to next time. I'll call you tonight before I go to bed?"

The feeling that I'm getting right now in my gut tells me to stop doubting this whole thing. My attraction to her is not based on how settled she is. It's based on who she is. The first night I met her, I knew I was crazy about her. And that was before I knew she had kids or that she was eight years older than me.

Who the fuck cares if I'm skipping to the good part? This woman has me smiling like never before with just one text message. Someone like that is worth taking a chance on. She and I can figure out all the other stuff later.

Until then, I make a mental vow to myself that I won't let anyone else get into my head and try to convince me this is a bad idea.

Because I know deep down, in my soul, that this is probably the best thing I've ever done.

Chapter Twenty-three

ERIN

"No, Charlie! Don't eat that!" I scream at the dog who is heading toward the spot where I just threw up on the carpet.

I've gotten some sort of stomach bug, and I didn't make it all the way to the bathroom in time. The kids are all still running around like crazy, and although I want to tell them to knock it off, I don't have the energy.

I get down on my hands and knees to clean up the mess while trying to stifle my gagging. Unfortunately, being a single mom means that I don't get any sick days.

I manage to make it through without tossing my cookies again, but it exhausts me so much I feel like I just ran a marathon.

Before I collapse on the couch, I check my phone, hoping for a text from Tanner. I heard from him this morning but not much since. Although I'm sure I wouldn't be much fun to talk to right now, it would be nice to hear his voice.

It's been about a week since I saw him last, and I'm already missing him like crazy. Okay, I was missing him the second that he walked out the front door. This whole every other weekend thing is hard, but I guess it gives me something to look forward to.

I should do a grocery order to get some easy things for the kids to eat, but my head is spinning so hard that I just want to doze for a while.

"Boys," I call. "Can you guys just sit down and watch a movie long enough for me to take a little nap?"

They all come in the living room and pile onto the couch, but I know better than to think that they are going to stay here the whole time.

"Chris," I say to the oldest. "Can you please make sure that Joey doesn't hurt himself for me? Please? I will really owe you one."

"Sure, Mom."

I'd call my dad and ask him to help, but he went on a hunting trip for the week, so I'm out of luck there. And I tried asking Judd to take the kids for the night, but when he heard I had a stomach bug, he was convinced that one of the kids would carry it right on over to his house.

Selfish prick.

Just as I start to drift off, I hear the boys talking about being hungry. I tell them that I will get up and fix dinner once I get back up—although everything about that idea makes me queasy.

A knock on the door interrupts any rest I was hoping to get. Feeling like a zombie, I pull myself off the couch and lumber toward the sound. When I swing it open, I'm convinced that I must be seeing things because Tanner stands in my doorway.

Clearly, I'm delirious from exhaustion.

"Tanner?" I ask.

"Hey, babygirl."

"What—what are you doing here? I thought you were out of town for a few more days."

He shrugs. "When you told me you were sick and having a hard time, I figured I could skip out a little early to come make sure you were okay. I brought supplies."

I didn't even notice that he has a couple of pizza boxes in one hand and some grocery sacks in the other.

Since I'm still trying to wrap my head around this whole thing, he says, "Look, I'm not asking for anything here. I really just came by to drop this off to help make things a little bit easier on you."

My mind still reels, and I guess I'm giving off the illusion that I'm angry.

"Shit," he says. "I should have asked first. I'm so sorry. I shouldn't have just come here with your kids home. I'll just leave this stuff on the porch and get out of here."

My eyes sting with tears because I've never had anyone do something so sweet for me. This man left his job and drove all the way home just to drop off stuff for my kids and I.

He frantically looks around for a place to set everything down.

"Tanner," I say.

He looks at me with worry in his eyes. "I'm so sorry. I really wasn't trying to push you."

"Tanner," I say again, this time taking a deep breath. "Would you like to come inside?"

"But your kids are home."

"I know." I try to pull out a smile, but I'm sure it probably looks ridiculous with how crappy I feel. "I'd like for you to meet my kids."

The smile that he gives is far larger than mine.

Maybe this is a bad idea, but my brain fog is convincing me otherwise.

"Only if you're sure," he says.

"I am."

He follows me inside the house, and all three boys turn to look at us.

"Boys, can you come here, please?"

They all do as I ask and come to stand in front of us.

"This is Tanner. He's a friend of mine." Pointing to each of them, I say, "This is Chris, Alex, and Joey."

Alex asks, "Are you two dating?"

Joey asks, "What is *dating*?"

Chris chimes in with, "It means he's sleeping with our mom."

"Christopher!" I scold.

Joey looks confused. "He came here to sleep?"

Chris laughs. "I doubt much sleeping will go on."

Alex's face scrunches up. "Ew."

Chris says, "No wonder she's been in such a good mood lately."

"That's it," I say. "I'm going to tell Tanner to take your pizza back because none of you deserve it."

"Pizza?" They all ask in unison.

Tanner asks, "Pepperoni and cheese okay?"

Joey starts running around the living room and jumping off the couch like Spiderman. "Cheese is the best!"

Tanner notices how I look like I may upchuck again at any moment at all the talk of greasy pizza, so he says, "Come on guys, let's take this to the kitchen and grab some."

"Boys," I tell them. "All of you better be on your *best* behavior, or when I get feeling better, there will be hell to pay."

They all nod and follow Tanner. I go to follow them, but instead, I find myself running toward the bathroom. I have no clue how I have anything left in my stomach to throw up, but apparently, there's something.

As I'm hugging the porcelain throne, I feel two large hands on my shoulders before one of them pushes the stray hairs out of my face.

"You don't need to see this," I tell Tanner. "You won't find me attractive anymore."

"Babygirl, I would think you're attractive no matter what. A little throw-up isn't going to scare me off."

"My kids might, though." I chuckle before the next round of heaving starts.

When I finish, Tanner gets a washrag and wets it before handing it to me to wipe my mouth. "Nah, I don't think they'll scare me off either. I used to be one of those crazy kids, so I know all the tricks. I have a leg up on them."

We walk back to the couch, and I lay at one end, trying to get comfortable. Tanner covers me up with a blanket and hands me the remote. I don't get very far into picking something to watch on Netflix before I fall asleep with the remote still in my hand.

When my eyes finally open again, I see something that makes me thinks I'm surely still dreaming.

Tanner with my three boys. All of them sitting around the coffee table with a Monopoly game going in the center. A Harry Potter movie is on the TV, and all of them look completely enthralled by what's happening on the screen.

I wasn't sure if inviting Tanner in was a good idea, but it looks like I had nothing to worry about. I try not to make any noise because I want to take in this moment without any interruptions.

Joey looks up at Tanner and pulls on his sleeve. "That dog has three heads."

"I know. His name is Fluffy."

Joey starts laughing. "That's a silly name for a dog with three heads."

My heart melts a little when something on the screen startles him, and he climbs into Tanner's lap.

How does this man have such unbelievable magnetism toward everyone he spends time with? I told myself that there was no way I was going to fall in love again, yet I felt comfortable with Tanner almost immediately. And now, my kids seem to like him, too. They aren't grilling him or being mean or difficult.

I half expected to wake up to Tanner duct taped to the chair while the boys destroyed the house. Don't get me wrong—I love my children. Overall, they're good kids, but when they get a chance to cause some mischief, they typically don't pass up the chance. After all, they are just little boys who are trying to have a good time.

But here they are. On their best behavior.

With the man that I love.

Whoa, did I really just think that?

I think I did.

And I think it's true.

I've been working so hard at keeping my two lives separate, never figuring that the two might fit together so seamlessly.

Chapter Twenty-four

TANNER

Okay, Erin's kids are great. Our meeting went far better than I ever could have expected. When Erin texted and told me she was sick and was worried about taking care of the kids, I thought helping out was the least that I could do.

Thankfully, the job I was on was just about over, and I thought the guys could handle things without me. When I called to tell my boss I was heading out early, I also told him that I needed a change. Being on the road so often isn't working for me anymore.

At first, he brushed it off and acted like he didn't want to hear it, but when I brought up the fact that I was getting poached by another local company, he changed his tune. Thank goodness because I can handle a little bit of travel, but the days of being gone two whole weeks at a time have to come to an end.

Maybe I'm counting my chickens before they hatch here, but I'd like to be home more for Erin. It's hard to put down roots when your feet aren't firmly on the ground. When I first started this job, the travel was only supposed to be temporary. I worked for John, my boss, when I was in high school, and he hired me full-time right after I graduated. His plan was to have me travel for a year or so and then transfer me into more of a managerial role. But one year has turned into almost seven. I'm ready for a change.

I plan on telling Erin all of this when she gets feeling better. Right now, her head is spinning enough without me dropping any big information on her.

I came here with the mere intent of dropping off some pizza and other supplies, so I was floored when Erin invited me in. The boys were all relatively quiet until their mom fell asleep, and then the questions started.

Alex asked, "Are you in love with my mom?"

"Yeah," I told him. "But I haven't told her that yet, so let's keep this between us boys, okay?"

They asked me what I did for work and what I liked to do for fun. I felt like I was on the most important job interview of my entire life.

Chris seemed the most hesitant to give me any type of a chance, but when we were alone in the kitchen together, he decided to open up a little. Turning to me, he says, "Look, I don't care what you and my mom do, but please promise me that you'll treat her right. My dad always treated her like shit, and she deserves better."

I'm completely shocked—not about the fact that a thirteen-year-old just used the word 'shit', but because this kid is able to see how his mom was treated. Guess it's true that kids pay attention more than you think they do.

I tell him, "I promise that I won't do anything to hurt her, and I'll do my best to treat her like the queen she is."

He crosses his arms over his chest. "Are you going to tell my mom I said shit?"

"I don't think she needs to know anything about it."

That gets a smile out of him. "Maybe you're not so bad."

Before he walks out of the room, I ask, "Hey, Chris, have you ever told your mom your feelings about how your dad treats her?"

He shakes his head. "What's the point? They got divorced."

Before I can say anything else, he walks out of the room. Probably a good thing. It's not my place to get in the middle of all that. And I should follow Erin's examples and not talk badly about the kids' dad in front of them.

An hour later, we all sit in the living room, playing Monopoly and watching Harry Potter. It didn't take much convincing for them to want to watch it with me. Chris said he had watched the first one in school a few years ago, and he liked it.

They've been entranced ever since. We've talked a little as I try to get to know them a little better.

Not only are they smart, but all three of them are hilarious. Erin was right. They're all great kids.

When a scary part comes on the movie, Joey climbs into my lap.

A month ago, I was prowling the bars in whatever town I was in and looking for someone to take home for the night. Now, I'm hanging out with my girlfriend's kids while we watch Harry Potter. I've dreamed of something like this for so long. Maybe it's not exactly in the way that I imagined it, but damnit, it's still perfect.

We all get so into the movie that we completely forget about the boardgame in front of us. When the credits roll, I realize that it's getting late, and I'm pretty sure the kids have school tomorrow.

Looking at Chris, I say, "What time do you guys normally go to bed?"

He looks at his phone. "About twenty minutes ago."

When he looks back at me and sees the fact that I'm not really sure what to do next, he says, "Come on guys. Let's go get ready for bed."

He picks a sleepy Joey up out of my arms and carries him upstairs. The way Chris is with his brothers reminds me a lot of Duke when we were younger. Although he was so much older than us, and he typically was always busy with his own stuff, he would watch us sometimes when our mom would go out. Half the time, he was more of a parent than she was. I'm glad Chris doesn't have to carry that burden because Erin is one hell of a mom.

As I'm cleaning up the living room and kitchen, Joey comes back downstairs. He's dressed in footy-pajamas and is carrying a stuffed rhino.

"Hey Joey, you okay?" I ask.

"I came to ask Momma to read me a story."

"Well, Momma's still sleeping."

His face falls. "Oh. Can you read to me?"

"Uh, sure."

He grabs my hand and leads me upstairs to his bedroom. Once there, he grabs a book about a friendly shark off the shelf, and I start reading to him. I'm so into doing voices and having fun with it that I don't even realize that Joey has fallen asleep. It isn't until Erin peeks her head in the doorway and points to him that I notice it.

As quietly as I can, I get up off the bed and shut off the light before exiting the room. Erin takes me by the hand and leads me to her bedroom. She still looks pale as a ghost and moves pretty slowly.

She lays down on the bed, and I climb next to her to pull her close.

"You're cold, babygirl," I tell her, reaching for the blanket to cover us both up.

"You're going to get sick," she says.

"Eh, worth it."

She nuzzles into my chest before saying, "Thank you for tonight. You really didn't have to come here and do all this. I don't know how to repay you."

"You don't repay me, beautiful. This is how this works. We have each other, no matter what. We help each other out when we need it."

"Still, I know three kids is a lot to take on."

I kiss the top of her head. "They're great kids."

"They're alright," she jokes. Sick as a dog and still funny as hell. "They seem to like you too. I guess now maybe you can come around more often—you know, when you're not working."

"About that," I tell her. "I may be in town a lot more often."

"Oh?" She asks, barely able to keep her eyes open.

"Yeah, but we will talk about it later."

"Okay, baby." She goes quiet for a minute but then says, "Hey, Tanner?"

"Yes, beautiful?"

"I love you."

An unexpected smile crosses my lips. Fuck, it feels good to hear her say those words. I don't even care that she's sick and possibly delirious when she said them.

Pulling her tighter, I say, "I love you too, babygirl. So fucking much."

As I look down, I see that she's already softly snoring against me. I guess I'll just have to tell her again tomorrow.

And every single day from now on that she will have me.

Chapter Twenty-five

ERIN

"Where does the pasta go?" Tanner asks me as we unload the grocery bags.

I point to the cabinet next to the microwave. "That one. Hey, thank you for watching the kids while I went to the store. It makes it way easier to go without six extra hands randomly throwing things in the cart."

'No worries. We went out back and kicked the soccer ball around for a while. I don't know who is more worn out—them or me."

"I'm sure they like having you around to play with. Running around doesn't bode well for women with big boobs. I about give myself a black eye."

"Not going to lie; I'd like to see that."

I laugh. "You just want to see them bounce."

"Duh." He walks over to me and puts his hands on my ass. "Maybe later on, I can see them bounce in a completely different context."

I smile. "I think we can arrange that."

He leans in to whisper, "Think you can be quiet?"

Lately, Tanner and I have always had the kids, so every time we get any *sexy* time, it's usually quick, and I have to try to be as quiet as a church mouse. Do you know how hard that is while a man with a cock ring screws your brains out?

After Tanner met the boys, I realized that I was silly for wondering how this would all work. So far, it's going great. Tanner got promoted at work, so he's around a lot more, which I love. And so do the kids.

This whole thing is working out much better than I ever thought it could have. Tanner still hasn't stayed the night with the kids home. I'm still a little iffy on that one and don't want to completely shell shock the kids. We will get there eventually.

For now, Tanner comes over after I get off work, and we spend the evening together with the kids. And now that it's my weekend to have the kids, he came over early this morning and is spending the day.

It's all wonderful, but I'm waiting for the other shoe to drop. There has to be something wrong with this, right? It's all too perfect to just stay that way.

He trails a few kisses along my neck, waiting for my answer as to whether or not I can keep quiet while he does filthy things to my naked body.

Running my fingers through his hair, I say, "I actually had another idea."

"What's that, beautiful?"

"Well, my friends called this morning, wanting to see what was going on tonight."

"Do you want me to watch the boys so you can go have a girl's night?" He asks as though that would be no big deal. Could this man be any more wonderful?

"Thank you for the offer, but I actually already asked my dad to watch the kids tonight. I thought we could go out together. We can spend some time with my friends and then come home and have some completely uninterrupted alone time."

His pierced tongue licks his bottom lip. "Oh, yeah?"

"Mm-hmm. And then, guess what?"

"What?"

Now, it's my turn to whisper in his ear. "I don't have to be quiet."

"You realize that I'm going to be thinking about that all day now, right?"

I lean up to kiss him. "Yep."

"God, I love you," he says before kissing me.

"I love you too."

The other night, when I was sick and told him I loved him, I meant it. Watching Tanner interact with my kids in such an amazing way was enough to make me say it out loud. The next day, Tanner said it to me, and I could tell he was nervous. He thought maybe I wouldn't remember, or maybe I didn't mean it.

But I meant it then, and I mean it now.

I never thought I would fall in love again, but the universe brought me Tanner—the one man I think that could rip down all the walls that I've built.

I do my best to drown out the little voice in my head that tells me another shoe will drop. It always does.

"Have I mentioned how stunning you look?" Tanner leans in to ask me.

Gina and Nancy got up to go to the bar and grab another round for all of us, leaving Tanner and I at the table alone.

"You have, but I don't think I'll get tired of hearing it."

"When we get home, I'm going to enjoy making you come every way imaginable."

Just the thought of it makes me wet. We've still had sex lately—great sex even. But I'm ready for him to fuck my brains out tonight.

When Nancy and Gina return, they bombard Tanner with questions. What are your intentions with our friend? How do you feel about Erin having kids? Do you have a criminal record?

I guess he answers all of their questions in an acceptable manner because they seem to lighten up on him. Gina even goes on to ask him a question about the guy she's been seeing.

"We seem to be getting along really well. But he always wants to come to my place. I have no idea where he lives. When I suggest coming over, he freaks out on me."

"How many times?" Tanner asks.

"We've been seeing each other for about a month now."

I'm a little shocked because Gina doesn't normally 'date'. She just adds notches to her bedpost. She's all about the fun, and it's always worked for her. So, it's a little weird that she's hung up on this guy.

Tanner asks, "And he won't even give you his address?"

I jump in. "To be fair, Tanner, I haven't seen your place. We always go to mine."

He chuckles. "That's because your place is way nicer than mine, but if you want to go see where I live, I have no problem with it. That's the difference here. This guy clearly doesn't want you seeing his place. Chances are, he has something to hide."

Gina asks, "What do you think it is?"

Tanner shrugs his shoulders. "I'm not sure, but if I had to guess, I'd say he's got another woman. I hate to be the one to say this, but it sounds like you're the side chick."

She takes a sip of her beer. "That's what I was afraid of."

"Sorry, Gina," I say.

"Eh, it's alright. I wasn't in love or anything. He was just a good lay. Guess all the good ones are taken." She smiles at Tanner and I.

"Damn straight," I say. "And I'm not giving this one up."

We talk a bit more before Tanner asks if I want to dance. I suck at dancing, but I'm anxious for a moment alone with him.

He leads me to the dancefloor, and I warn, "Just letting you know that I'm not very good at this."

He puts his hands on my hips, and says, "Just follow my lead. Sway with the music."

Country music blares through the speakers, and I let Tanner control my movements. My hands link around his neck as we dance to the beat. He's so sexy, and I can feel a ton of eyes on us. I'm sure it's a bunch of women all wondering what a guy like him is doing with a woman like me.

He doesn't notice a single one of them, though. All he sees is me. And the way he looks at me makes me feel like I'm the most gorgeous woman in the world.

I lean up to kiss him. Taking a little bit of control, I slip my tongue in his mouth as we make out for a couple minutes.

When I pull back, he growls, "If you keep doing that, I'm taking you in the bathroom and fucking you."

Wanting to drive him even more crazy, I ask, "What if I do this?" I turn my body around and grind my ass against him.

"Erin," he warns.

"Hmm?" I ask, trying to act innocent.

"Alright, as much fun as this has been, I think it's about time I take you home and show you a good time."

Don't have to ask me twice.

I grab his hand and begin to lead him out of the bar. We stop by to tell Nancy and Gina that we are heading out before making our way to the door. The second we are outside, Tanner pushes me up against the brick wall of the building, pinning my arms above my head and kissing me.

It's so hot, but I want more. I *need* more.

Just when I about to break the kiss and tell him get me home as quickly as possible, I hear something that makes my stomach turn.

"Erin, what the hell do you think you're doing?"

Judd.

Hear that? It's the other shoe dropping.

Chapter Twenty-Six

TANNER

When Erin's ex-husband calls her name, her entire demeanor changes. The woman who was just so confidant and sure of herself suddenly disappears into her shell.

"Judd?" She asks. "What are you doing here?"

"I think the better question is what are *you* doing here? Where the fuck are my children?"

"They're with my dad," she says.

"So, you just dump the kids off at your dad's and come here to hang out with…" He looks over at me. "The help?"

I bite my tongue because I know that anything rude I say is just going to make things harder on Erin. So, I just hold out my hand and say, "Hi, I'm Tanner. I'm Erin's boyfriend."

He looks at my hand with nothing but disdain before his gaze falls on Erin. "Boyfriend? When were you going to tell me? Weren't you just giving me shit about Mary Louise? Clearly, you had someone waiting in the wings."

"Judd," she begins, but he doesn't give her the chance to speak.

"Imagine my surprise when I get a phone call that my ex-wife, and the mother of my children, is at the local watering hole, making a slut out of herself."

I can't keep quiet anymore. "Hey, if you're pissed, that's fine, but we don't need to do the name calling."

"I don't think I was talking to you, son. How about you let the adults speak?"

Anger boils my blood. I'm trying to be civil, but this guy is just going way too far.

Erin speaks before I have the chance to, though. "Judd, please stop."

"No, Erin, you stop. Stop acting like you don't have kids at home waiting for you. On my weekends, do you see Mary Louise and I going out and dry humping each other on the dance floor? No. Because I take the time with my children seriously. And I believe in a thing called modesty. No woman of mine would ever be caught dancing like that."

Not able to contain my smart-ass tongue, I say, "Maybe you're just not doing it right."

He looks back at Erin. "Are you really bringing this guy around the kids? I should have known that something like this would happen. I should have known that once we divorced, you'd go right back to being the little slut that you were before we met."

I can see the tears gleaming in her eyes. I want to haul off and punch Judd, but Erin grabs my hand, signaling me to calm down.

He leans in close to her face and says, "If you are going to keep pulling shit like this, I will take you back to court so fast. I'm sure the judge would be interested to hear about your extracurricular activities."

He walks away, and Erin stands there still as stone for a moment before saying through a shaky voice, "Can we go now?"

I realize their argument drew a crowd, so I get her through the swarm of people and out to my truck. Stepping on it, I try to get back to her place as soon as possible. It's a quiet ride because quite frankly, I have no idea what to say.

From what I have seen of Erin, she is strong and independent. She has been through some rough shit, and it's made her tougher. But Judd's presence turns her into someone completely different. It makes me wonder how much psychological damage Judd really did to her.

When we get back to her place, both of us make our way to the kitchen. Erin pulls out two water bottles from the fridge and hands me one.

"I'm sorry you had to see that," she says. "I tend to forget that Judd has little spies around town."

Without thinking about it, I say, "Why do you let him talk to you like that?"

Her eyes dart up to look at me. "What should I do, Tanner?"

"I don't know. Tell him exactly when and where to fuck off?"

"And how would that make things better for my kids? How would any of that make this divorce any easier?" Her voice is laced with annoyance.

"Erin," I begin.

"No, Tanner. This whole situation sucks. You know what? I can deal with Judd calling me a slut. What I can't deal with is him taking any of his frustration about me out on the kids. Why do you think I stuck around for so long? Why do you think I let him treat me like dirt? Because I wanted to keep things calm for my children. I would do anything for them. I would fucking die for them."

I walk over and grab either side of her face. "Hey, I know. It's okay. I'm sorry I even brought it up. But you have to understand how hard it is for me to hear someone talk about you like that."

She takes a deep breath. "I know. I just need you to let me handle Judd in my own way. Please. I'm just trying to keep the peace."

"Do you really think he would try to take the kids?"

She rolls her eyes. "Probably not. As much as Judd loves his kids, I don't think he wants them full-time. Heck, he didn't want them full-time when he lived with them. The only reason he would ever even try would be out of spite for me."

"Are you worried about it?"

She lets out a heavy sigh. "Tanner, I'm always worried about it. And I don't mean that I'm just worried about him taking the kids. I mean that I'm worried about how he's going to respond or react to things."

"It just pisses me off that he calls you a slut. You're anything but that. What was he going on about?"

After taking a long drink of water, she says, "Back in high school, before Judd and I got together, I was headed down a different path. I was partying a lot and fooling around with anyone who would have me. I wasn't sleeping with them, but I was doing everything else. When I got with Judd, he made it very clear that my lifestyle was going to need to change. Whenever we would get into a really heated fight, he would bring up the idea that he 'saved me' or something. Like he did some huge favor by saving me from myself."

What do you know? Another reason for me to hate this guy.

I pull her close to me again. "For what it's worth, I don't care what you've done in your past. And I promise to never talk to you like that."

"I know." She smiles.

"How about you and I go upstairs, and I try to help you forget about this night?"

I wonder if she will actually say yes because if I was her, I'm not sure I would be in the mood for sex right now.

But she surprises me once again by taking me by the hand and leading me up the stairs.

Time to get that asshole out of her mind.

The next morning, Erin and I lie in bed together. I think we are still reeling a bit from the night before, but neither one of us are bringing it up.

My phone rings on the table next to me, and I pick it up and see that it's my mother and immediately reject the call.

"Everything okay?" Erin asks.

"Yeah, it's just my mom."

"You can talk to her if you want. I won't get upset or anything."

I kiss the top of her head. "I know. I'm a little pissed at her."

"Oh? Why?"

I seriously consider whether or not I want to tell Erin the conversation that I had with my mother. I don't want Erin to necessarily have a bad opinion of my momma to start with, but then again, my mother already seems to have a bad opinion of Erin. So, fuck it.

"I went over to see her one day, and she pretty much told me how I should rethink getting with a woman with three kids."

Erin's face falls. "Oh."

"She thinks that I am just trying to jump to the end without going through the journey. She doesn't want me to settle."

"Do you think you're settling?" She asks in a quiet voice.

"Hey, look at me. I don't think that at all. I'm happy as fuck that I'm with you, and I'm not going anywhere."

I look at her and see tears in her eyes. "Even after what happened with Judd?"

"That man can try his hardest to scare me off, but I'm in love with you, Erin. I'm not leaving. You're the best thing that's ever happened to me."

I mean everything that I'm saying. I'm crazy about this woman, and I have no intention of letting her go. But I figure it's as good a time as any to ask a couple of questions.

"Erin, do you want to get married again?"

Her eyes go wide. "Is that some sort of proposal? Because if it is, you're doing it wrong."

I laugh. "No... not yet anyway. I just realize that we haven't exactly talked about some of the big stuff."

She thinks for a moment. "I wouldn't mind getting married again, but it has to be right." She pauses for a moment before adding, "And before you ask, I don't know if I want any more kids. If you would have asked me a year ago, I would have told you that I was ready to get my tubes tied, but now, I'm not so sure."

"What's changing your mind?" I ask. "Or potentially changing your mind."

"Well, this past month has showed me that nothing is as sure as I thought it was. I realize that I don't know quite what the universe has in store for me, and maybe I should be open to anything."

My phone interrupts us again, but I see this time it is Duke, not my mother. Although I normally wouldn't answer, Duke NEVER calls me. Ever. He is the epitome of radio silence most of the time.

"It's Duke," I say before putting the phone to my ear and answering. "Hello?"

"Hey, Tanner, what's going on?"

"Uhhh, not much. You okay? You never call me."

I hear Avery in the background say, "See? I told you that you were going to freak people out by calling them."

"Oh, hush," he tells her before turning his attention back to me. "Everything is great, actually. Next weekend, Avery and I have decided to tie the knot."

"No shit? Congratulations, man."

"Thank you. I thought it was time I make an honest woman out of her." Next, I hear, "Ouch, Avery don't hit me. I was just kidding."

It's so weird seeing my super stoic brother having a sense of humor.

He says, "Anyway, it's going to be a really small thing here at our house. I'd love for you to come. And Mom says you're dating someone now. I'd love for you to bring her too."

"Uh, yeah. I'd love to be there. I'll have to check with Erin, but if she's free, I will bring her too. Just let me know what time."

We say our goodbyes, and Erin sits wide-eyed, waiting to hear what I have to say.

"Duke and his girl, Avery, are getting married next weekend. We've both been invited."

"Oh, well, that's nice."

I realize that maybe I shouldn't have volunteered Erin to go without talking to her first. "Shit, I'm sorry, Erin. If you don't want to go, I will just say that you're busy with the kids. No big deal. I don't want you to feel weird being around my mom or anything."

She gently squeezes my hand. "I'd love to go with you."

Chapter Twenty-seven

ERIN

"Tanner, are you going to come to my game tonight?" Alex asks. "I want to try to do one of those bicycle kicks that we've been working on."

Before Tanner can say a word, I interject. "Oh, sweetie, I don't think Tanner can make it tonight. He has to go out of town for work tomorrow, and we don't want to keep him out too late."

Alex just gives a sad, "Oh," and walks back out of the room.

Tanner looks at me. "Hey, it's no big deal for me to go to his game. I'd love to see him play. And I'll only be gone for one night. I'll be okay if I miss a little sleep."

"I know," I say. "I just think it would probably be better if I went to the game alone."

"Want to tell me why?"

I wipe down one of the counters in the kitchen while explaining, "Well, Judd will be there, and—"

"And you don't want him and me in the same place?"

"Something like that."

He walks toward me and grabs my hand. "You know that if you and I are going to make this work, eventually, he and I will have to coexist, right? I don't want to miss every single function that the kids have just because Judd is going to be there."

"I know," I tell him. "I just haven't figured out the best way to handle this yet."

"Maybe tell him to put on his big boy pants and deal with it?"

My eyes narrow in on him. "You and I both know it isn't that easy."

"Is Mary Louise going to be there?"

"I don't know," I say. Not wanting to lie, I add, "Probably."

"Then, I don't see why he should care."

Sighing, I say, "Neither do I, Tanner. But I'm trying to keep the peace here. It's Alex's soccer game. I really don't want there to be drama."

"I know," he mumbles. "I'm sorry. It's just frustrating."

Honestly, after how Judd acted the other night, I'm surprised Tanner is still here. I figured Judd's asshole nature would have scared him right off. I have a sinking feeling of dread, though, that Tanner isn't going to stick around if I keep making excuses like this.

Do I want Judd and Tanner to get along?

Sure.

Do I have any idea how to make that happen?

Nope.

Do I want to try to figure it out at my son's soccer game where Judd will make a huge scene?

Absolutely not.

"I know it's frustrating," I tell him, wrapping my arms around my neck. "I'm sorry. I promise that I will find a way to make this whole thing work. Just give me a little bit of time. Please."

He gives a silent nod.

"And when you get back, you can come over, and I'll try to help make it better." I lean up and kiss him.

"It's not fair when you do that, you know," he says. "It makes me want to forget that I'm upset."

"Oh, really?"

"Yeah," he says, moving away from me. "Look, I'm going to go talk to Alex real quick before I head out. I don't want him to be mad at me."

Guilt washes over me. Tanner has been there for these kids so much in the short time since knowing them. On nights when we are all home, he helps with homework, reads stories, cooks dinner, and just hangs out with them. He's the husband I always pictured myself having. He's helping out with three kids that he didn't create. The guy who did create them is actively trying to make our lives hell.

And here I am, making it easier for Judd to do that.

I'm just not sure what else to do. The other day when Judd took the boys out for dinner, he made sure to give me hell when he brought them home. He made all the same threats he was making at the bar, telling me that I'm lucky he doesn't take the boys from me.

If Judd took me back to court, which I highly doubt he would, it's unlikely he would get full custody. But I never want it to even get to that point. I never want my kids to have to go through that again. After the first time, I was convinced they were going to need therapy for the rest of their lives. The divorce was ugly. Phone conversations were recorded, bank accounts were analyzed, and even some visits were supervised. The whole thing was a mess, and it put so much stress on the kids that I wasn't sure they would come out of it.

They did. Eventually. But it took a couple of months. I don't want them to have to worry like that anymore.

For that reason, I take all the bullshit that Judd dishes out. Better me than them.

And I love Tanner, but I don't know if I'm going to be able to keep him and keep the peace that I have achieved.

I have no idea what Tanner says to Alex. I didn't want to go in and listen and somehow make this whole situation worse.

When Tanner comes back in, I say, "You don't have to rush off."

"Yeah, I do," he replies. "You guys have a game to get to."

I ask, "Do you still want me to come to the wedding with you this weekend?"

"Of course," he says matter-of-factly.

I'm relieved that he still kisses me before he leaves, but I still feel awful about everything that happened. I didn't mean to hurt his feelings. Tanner is just like a golden retriever, and I feel like the monster that just stepped on his tail.

I should have known that this whole thing was going to be hard. Everything was way too perfect, and I knew the other shoe would drop.

I have to find a way to make this up to him—a way to make it right because I don't want to lose him. Eventually, me kissing him or getting naked just isn't going to cut it anymore.

"Good job, Alex! Way to go, buddy!" Mary Louise yells as the soccer game plays out in front of us. After a while, her voice starts to sound like nails on a chalkboard. But she's trying to be nice, so I keep my mouth shut.

Every time I say anything at all—even something to my other two kids—Judd feels the need to mutter something under his breath. I can't hear exactly what he's saying, but Chris sits right next to his dad, and I'm sure he's hearing all of it.

Part way through the second half, Chris jumps up off the bleachers and says, "Enough!" He turns to me and says, "Mom, I'm going to go wait by the car."

Before I can ask what's going on, he storms off.

Judd's head snaps toward me. "Look what you've done."

"What could I have possibly done? I wasn't even talking to him. You were. What did you say to him?"

"It's none of your business what I say to *my* son."

"Okay, Judd," I say with a sigh. "Whatever."

He gets up to go after Chris, but I don't let him get far before I stop him. "What are you doing?"

"I'm going to get him. He can come back here and watch his brother's game."

"No, you're not," I tell him. "He needs a minute. Let him cool off."

With his hands on his hips, Judd starts pacing. Pointing his finger at me, he says, "You're the reason he's turning into such a little shit."

"Judd, he's a teenager. They're all little shits."

He cringes when he hears me use the same language as him. "He's become so disrespectful lately."

"Are we talking about the same kid?" I ask. "I think you're overreacting a little."

"I think you're doing your best to turn him against me."

"What?" Wasn't this the same guy who was just talking about me in front of our kid on the bleachers? "Judd, I never say a bad word about you in front of the kids."

"Bullshit!" He raises his voice, causing a couple of people to look over at us. "I can tell you this—if Chris lived with me, he wouldn't have this attitude problem. You're too soft on him. He needs a quick kick in the pants."

"What do you want me to punish him for?" I ask. "He didn't do anything wrong."

"See? That's the problem. You think his behavior is acceptable.

Before I can say anything else, he points his finger at me and says, "You don't want to mess with me, Erin. Trust me."

With that, he walks away. Thankfully, he doesn't continue walking toward the parking lot. He heads back over to sit with Mary Louise and finish watching the game. I take this opportunity to try to get some answers.

Quickly, I walk to the parking lot and see Chris leaning against the hood of my SUV.

When I reach him, I say, "Hey, kid."

"Hi." He kicks some dirt on the ground but doesn't look up at me. "I'm sorry I stormed off like that."

"It's alright. Just wanted to come make sure you were okay."

"I'm fine."

"Do you want to talk about what made you snap?"

Still no eye contact. "Not really."

"Okay," I move next to him. "Look, I know your dad can be a bit much sometimes."

He interrupts. "You don't know the half of it."

"No, I guess not. But you just have to learn to pick your battles."

That gets him to look at me. "And what battles do you actually pick?"

"Chris," I say, sternly.

"Just don't," he says. "Let's just go watch the rest of the game."

But as we are walking back, Alex comes towards us. "Where were you?! You missed my goal!"

Great.

Anybody else I want to piss off or disappoint today?

Chapter Twenty-eight

TANNER

"You look gorgeous," I tell Erin as I look over at her sitting in the passenger's seat.

"Thanks," she says, looking down at her sundress. "I wasn't sure exactly how fancy this wedding was going to be."

I chuckle. "Knowing Duke, not fancy at all. When you meet him, you'll see that Duke is the epitome of a simple man."

"Do you think your mom is going to be mean to me?" She asks nervously.

Grabbing her hand, I link my fingers with hers. "Not on my watch, she's not. And after spending five minutes with you, they'll all fall in love—just like I did."

A small smile tugs at her lips, but I can tell she's still anxious. That's further proven when she raises her other hand to her mouth and starts biting her nubby fingernails.

The past few days between us have been more than a little tense. The other night when she stopped me from going to Alex's game, my feelings were hurt. I probably shouldn't have reacted as harshly as I did. Afterwards, I tried putting myself in Erin's position, and no matter which way I thought about it there was never an easy answer.

The next day, I went out of town for work. John now has me just checking on completed jobs and giving the final okay so that we can move on to the next one. Instead of being gone for almost two weeks at a time, I'm maybe gone one or two days out of those two weeks. It's definitely been a lot easier, but it's still hard to head out of town when you feel like there's something hanging over the two of you.

Since I didn't get home until late, this is the first time that we've seen each other since. I'm sure it also doesn't help matters that we haven't gotten any *sexy* time since the bar incident. And even then, things were tense. Between having the kids and navigating our schedules, it's been hard to find the time to get down and dirty. I find that sometimes, when neither one of you knows the right thing to say, a long, hard fuck can help diffuse the tension.

Maybe it's not the healthiest way to deal with things, but I can only assume it's better than ignoring the problem.

What the hell do I know? I'm no therapist.

Hopefully, today, we can try to get back to where we were. The kids are with Judd, so she and I have the whole weekend together—assuming she wants me around that long.

When I first picked her up, she was walking on eggshells like she was terrified that I was still mad. Clearly, when Judd got mad about things, he *stayed* mad about things. I don't want to be that guy, and I don't want Erin ever thinking that she needs to be scared around me. The damage that has been done to her over the years runs deep.

I've been trying to compliment her and joke around so that she knows I'm not upset. Well, maybe that's not true. I'm upset but not necessarily at her. She's in an awful situation and is just trying to make everyone happy. I don't think anyone quite knows how to do that. As much as I want to tell her to go off on Judd and to give him all the hell that he deserves, she has to be ready to do it. Me forcing her to do something is no better than all the shit that Judd made her do for years.

The ride to Duke and Avery's is a short one, so I don't start any type of heavy conversation. Instead, I just try putting her at ease so that she has a good time at the wedding. When I pull into the long driveway, I see that we are the last ones to arrive. Devon's truck is already here, along with my mom's. I still haven't talked to my mother since our little altercation at her house. She's tried reaching out, but I haven't been in the mood to deal with it. I probably should have at least called her and asked that she be on her best behavior.

Oh well. Too late now.

The front door is open, so I hold Erin's hand as we walk inside. It looks like everyone is already out back. When we get out the back door, my whole family turns around to look. Erin squeezes my hand so hard it actually hurts.

Trying to break the tension, I say, "Hey everyone. The favorite child is here. Duke, you can go ahead and get married now."

That seems to make everyone laugh and go back to their business. Well, everyone except my mother who is now making a beeline toward us.

When she reaches us, she says, "Son, you've been avoiding my phone calls. I've been wanting to talk to you."

"Later," I tell her. "Today is about Duke. We aren't going to ruin that for him."

Still holding Erin's hand, I lead her around my mother and over to the chairs that are set up on the lawn.

Duke comes over and surprises me with a hug. When did my brother start hugging?

He and Avery both introduce themselves to Erin, and of course, Avery is just as sweet as she always is, which I'm grateful for. It appears to put Erin at ease at least a little bit.

Devon is next to come over and talk to us. I'm surprised that Kyra is with him. Knowing most of us don't like her, she usually avoids any Samson gatherings like the plague.

I'm tempted to be my typical smart-ass self and make a couple of snide remarks toward her. But I think better of it. I want people to be nice to Erin, and I should probably practice what I preach.

A few minutes later, the ceremony starts. I'm shocked to learn that they are going to read their own vows. It floors me that he was able to find the words and write them down; it surprises me even more that he's going to read them in front of all these people.

"Avery," he begins. "When I met you, I was completely closed off to any type of relationship. But the second you came into my life, all of that changed. I quickly changed from worrying that I wasn't good enough for you to making sure that I would be. You were my light through all the darkness I had endured. I promise to spend the rest of my life trying to be that same light for you. I know I'm a hell of a handful. Sometimes, I'm cranky or irritable. Some days, I'm just a plain asshole. But you're always there... no matter what. You are always in my corner, ready to throw down for me. I promise to always do the same for you. It's you and I against the world, sweetheart."

Avery looks at my brother with tears in her eyes. She looks down at the piece of paper in her hands and then crumples it up. "Everything I had written down is crap," she says with a chuckle. "Duke, you may be an asshole, but you're *my* asshole. I know you've been through so much in your life, and I don't presume to truly understand any of it. But the one thing I do understand is how to be here for you through it all. Being that person is a greater joy than I ever could have imagined. And I promise to be that person for you for the rest of our lives."

I wrap my arm around Erin's shoulders, and she nestles herself against me. Listening to Avery and Duke reminds me of what Erin and I have—although the roles are reversed. I want to be the person that is there for her no matter what. I want to be the pillar that she leans on for strength.

I guess I just need to have the strength and grace that my brother talked about. I need to check my ego at the door and realize how hard this whole thing is for her.

Chapter Twenty-nine

ERIN

Although I don't know much about Duke and Avery, their wedding was lovely. Tanner's whole family seems wonderful. Everyone has gone out of their way to come and talk to me—except Tammy, Tanner's mother. But as I stand in the kitchen, getting us something to drink, I think I'm about to get my chance. Tammy is heading in here, and she looks like a woman on a mission.

I really have no desire to talk to this woman right now because apparently, she's not a big fan of mine. Oh well. I'm used to moms not liking me. Judd's hated me until the day she passed away. I'm pretty sure she thought I was a terrible wife and resented me for 'ruining her son's life'. If only she knew what type of man she raised.

I take a deep breath as I wait for impact.

She comes in and makes her way over to the drink station where I'm standing. "Hi, there, dear," she greets.

"Hi," I reply as warmly as I can.

"So, you're the woman who has scooped up my son."

I'm not sure if that's a question of a statement, so I just say, "Yeah, I guess so."

"Look—" she begins, but I try to head her off at the pass.

"Before you say anything else, let me just say that I love your son. He's the best man I could ask for. I can only assume part of that is from the great job you did raising him." Some ass kissing never hurts. "I know that he and I dating doesn't make a whole lot of sense, but I'm crazy about him."

She gives me a forced smile. "As happy as I am to hear that, I still worry."

"About what?" I ask, showing the annoyance that I'm feeling.

"My youngest son has a heart of gold. Out of all of my sons, he loves the absolute hardest. For years, he's talked about wanting to find the right woman and put down some roots. I worry that maybe he's so eager to skip to the end that he's just settling."

Okay, now, I feel quite offended. "Yes, Tammie, I have three kids, but that doesn't mean that I'm *using* your son or just trying to get something out of it. I don't need him to be my sugar daddy or something."

She laughs. "It's not the *sugar* part I worry about. It's the *daddy.*"

"My kids have a father," I defend. "I'm not looking for someone to fill that role. As far as I'm concerned, my kids can never have enough people who care about them."

"Just be sure that you are bringing the right kind of people around your kids. Just because they claim to have good intentions doesn't mean they do."

I shake my head, trying to wrap my head around what she's trying to say. "So, should I be worried about your son around my kids or not? Because one second, you're defending him, and the next, you're telling me to watch my back."

She sighs. "Darlin', I love my son. Believe me when I say that I made every mistake in the book while raising him. That includes bringing around a whole lot of guys who had no intention of sticking around."

"You don't think your son will stick around?"

"I think he will do his best. I think either he will regret his decision and eventually walk away, or he will stay because he's a good man, but it would lead to him eventually resenting you."

Before I can say anything else, I hear Tanner's voice. Our conversation was so heated that I didn't even hear him come in. "Neither of those things is going to happen."

He walks over and puts his arm around my waist before continuing. "Here's how this is going to go. I love this woman. She's part of my life now. You can either jump on board with that and put on a smile, or you can get used to the fact that I won't come around as much."

"Tanner, I'm just saying—"

"No, Momma. You've said enough. Come on, Erin. Let's go say bye to Avery and Duke and get out of here."

The truck ride is another quiet one. I knew Tammie wasn't going to be a fan of mine, but I didn't think she would corner me and try to convince me how terrible of an idea this whole thing is.

I'm so preoccupied in my own thoughts that I don't even realize until Tanner parks the truck that we aren't at my house.

"Where are we?" I ask.

"I thought it was about time you saw my place." He smiles at me.

"Oh, okay."

He leads me inside, and my jaw drops. The only way I can describe it is a nerd's paradise. There's framed posters all over the walls, a huge shelf with movies and music, and a gaming computer with a fancy chair. My thirteen-year-old would never want to leave this place.

"Wow," I say.

It suddenly hits me that this man is only twenty-five. No matter how mature he may seem, Tanner is only twenty-five, and he's living exactly like a twenty-five-year-old should.

And I'm asking him to take on a mom and her three kids. That's a hell of a burden for someone.

Tanner notices my change in demeanor and says, "Hey, what's wrong? Are you not happy that I brought you here?"

"No, I love that you brought me here. But it's just making me think that maybe we are in different places in our lives."

He looks taken back. "What the hell does that mean?"

"I mean, I'm doing the mom thing, and you're living inside of a Best Buy." I start pacing around the room. "Maybe this is just the final nail in the coffin of why this whole thing is a bad idea."

He holds his hand up. "Whoa, whoa, whoa. You're going to have to back up ten steps. What were the first *nails in the coffin?*"

"Number one, Judd. Number two, your mother. Both of them seem to be determined to make sure this thing fails."

"Erin, one of them is your ex-husband who I'm pretty sure is going to hate anything you do regardless of what it is. And the other one is my mother—a woman who suddenly wants to find her maternal instinct when her kids are grown and out of the house. She's trying to make up for all of her shitty decisions. I don't put weight in either of what those two people say."

I take a deep breath. "It's just... look around. You are only twenty-five. You're able to spend your money on video games and motorcycles. I can't do that, but I don't want to take any of it away from you."

I can see that now, I'm getting a rise out of him. "Erin, why the fuck do you think I bought this stuff? Yes, it's cool, but I got it because I was fucking lonely. I was waiting for someone to come along and—".

I cut him off. "And I came along and pulled you into my shit show."

He runs his hands through his hair. "You're being impossible right now; do you know that?"

"How, Tanner? How am I being impossible?" I hear myself getting emotional, but after all of the stress of the last week, I can't help it.

"Because there's something that you just don't get. I would give up everything in this room if it meant I got to be with you. Fuck it all. Why do you think I'm always over at your house? Don't you think if I cared more about this stuff, I would spend more time at home? Yes, I have spent a lot of money on stupid shit. I get it. And you know what? Yes, I will probably spend money on stupid shit in the future, but you want to know the difference? I'll spend money on you and those kids. You talk about wanting to travel? Let's take a trip. Anywhere you want to go—I'll make it happen."

"I'm not asking you for that," I tell him.

"I know, babygirl. But don't you get it? You don't have to ask me to. I *want* to. I'm here, Erin. And I'm trying. Fuck, I'm trying so hard. Do you know how hard it is to keep my mouth shut when I hear Judd calling you a slut? Or when Alex asks me to go to a soccer game, and I'm told I'm not allowed to?"

Tears unexpectedly sting my eyes. "I don't want to hurt you."

He walks over to me and puts his hands on either side of my face. "When will you get it? I fucking love you. If all of that other shit is part of the package, I'll gladly take it. But for fuck's sake, I need you to stop pushing me away. I'm telling you I'm all in."

Tears now streak my cheeks. "I love you too."

I get the words out just as Tanner's lips crash down on mine. In between kisses, I ask, "What about everyone who thinks this thing is a bad idea?"

"Fuck everyone else," he growls.

Never taking his lips off mine, he walks me over to the kitchen and lifts me up onto the kitchen counter. His fingers slide underneath the dress I'm wearing and push my panties out of the way to give them easier access. His tongue dances with mine while he pushes to digits inside. I moan against his lips as he plays with that sweet spot.

His other hand lightly grabs my hair and tugs, pulling my head back so that he can kiss and bite my neck. I reach between my thighs to rub my clit, bringing myself to a quick orgasm.

When Tanner removes his fingers, he moves them to my lips. "Lick," he commands. "Taste how sweet this pussy is."

I do as he says, sucking on his fingers like I would his dick, and it drives him crazy. "Bedroom, now!" He orders.

I walk to where I assume the bedroom is, taking off my dress along the way. Before we get inside, Tanner pushes me against the wall, holding my hands above my head and kissing me.

Moments later, he's still kissing me, but now slowly walking me to the bedroom. Before I get on the bed, he takes the time to remove my bra and panties. Lying naked and waiting for him, I watch him quickly pull off his clothes before going to grab a condom.

"Hey," I stop him. "Come here."

"But—"

"You don't need it."

Crawling on the bed between my legs, he asks, "Are you sure?"

I nod. "I want to feel you without it."

And holy shit, it feels incredible.

Tanner and I have had a lot of sex, but this is something more special than anything we've shared. Not only is there nothing between us physically, but it feels like some of the emotional walls that were still up have come crashing down.

He makes love to me while still making me come over and over. We get lost in each other all night long, and it's enough to make me forget about all the obstacles standing in our way.

At least until tomorrow.

Chapter Thirty

TANNER

"Hello?" I answer the phone through the speakers in my truck. I've been trying to ignore my mother since we saw her a week and half ago at the wedding, but she just won't give up.

"Hey there, darlin'."

"What do you want, Momma?" I ask, still rather annoyed with her.

"I guess we are just skipping past the pleasantries, huh?"

"You verbally attacked my girlfriend. You're lucky I'm talking to you at all."

"Well, if you would have answered your phone, you would have known before now that maybe I'm ready to eat some crow."

I pause for a second. "Go on."

"Rob helped me see that maybe I was being a bit hasty. If you love Erin, I should probably try to give her a chance."

The way she says the words makes me think that Rob is standing right there, watching her and making sure she's being civil.

She goes on to say, "Maybe you two can come over for dinner one night, and we can get to know Erin a little bit better."

She says the words as though she's getting her teeth pulled or something.

"I don't know. We will have to see. Erin has the kids most of the time," I tell her.

"They're welcome to come," she offers.

"Probably best if we do dinner without the kids first. Let you get any of the bullshit out that's left in your system."

She exhales a heavy sigh. "I'm trying here, son. Can you meet me half way?"

"Let me talk to Erin, and I'll get back to you."

"Oh, that sounds promising," she says in her most sarcastic voice.

"Unlike you, Momma, Erin is extremely open-minded, and I bet you anything she will be more up for going to dinner than I am."

She says something else, but I don't hear what it is because I see red and blue lights pop up behind me. I pull over to get out of the cop's way, but much to my surprise, he pulls to the side of the road right behind me.

I know I wasn't speeding, so I wonder what this whole thing is about.

"Momma, I have to go."

Before she can say anything else, I hang up the phone.

My eyes stay fixed in the rearview mirror to see what's going on.

"Son of a bitch," I mutter as I see who's getting out of the police car.

Judd.

The gift that just keeps on giving.

As he gets to me, I roll my window down. "Can I help you, officer?" I ask, trying to be civil.

"License and registration."

I reach into my wallet, and with his hand on his gun, he says, "What are you doing there, boy?"

"Getting my wallet. You going to shoot me for it?"

Both of us stare at each other, waging some silent war. I grab him what he needs and hands it to him. "What was I doing?"

"Speeding," he replies while looking at my license.

"Bullshit," I blurt. "I was driving behind Mrs. Higgens. She's 83 years old. There's no way anyone can speed behind her."

"Are you arguing with me?" He asks while slowly chewing his gum.

This guy is a grade A prick.

"Just telling you the facts."

"Well, how about we take this conversation to the station?"

I laugh.

"Something funny, boy?"

"How old are you to where you feel the need to call me boy? Must be getting pretty far up there, huh?"

Shut up, Tanner.

I hear the voice in my head, but my mouth doesn't get the memo.

He takes off his sunglasses and looks at me. "Well, your girlfriend is the same age as me, so what does that say about you?"

"From what I hear, your girlfriend is even younger than I am."

"Step out of the car, boy."

Five minutes later, I'm in cuffs in the back of Judd's cop car. I just couldn't keep my mouth shut. And this asshole was looking for any reason in the world to stick it to me.

And of course, I gave him one.

"I'm not sure you understand that you're playing with fire here, boy," Judd says from the front seat.

"Why do you care what Erin and I do?" I ask.

"Because that woman has custody of my children. I will do everything I can to make sure that's a good environment for them."

"Why do you assume that I would ruin that?"

"Just look at you, boy. Piercings. Tattoos. Hair like a girl. No sons of mine are going to grow up and be like you."

I don't say anything else because what's the point? I'm just going to piss this guy off more, and he's likely to frame me for murder or something.

When we get to the station, he sticks me in a cell for a couple of hours until I'm allowed to make my phone call. I consider calling Erin, but I'm not sure I want her to know about this whole encounter. I don't know how pissed off she would be at me, and honestly, she doesn't need the extra stress.

So, I call Duke.

One thing about my brother... a lot of people around town are scared of him. It's not just his big, burly appearance, but when he was a teenager, he committed a crime in self-defense. People always worried about what else he may do.

I figure having him pick me up might work in my favor somehow.

It's less than twenty minutes before my brother comes storming through the door. "Where the hell is my brother?" He asks the officer at the desk.

"Who's your brother?"

"Don't play me. In this small town, everyone knows everyone. Tanner Samson. I want to see him. Now."

"You'll need to pay his bail."

"Bail?" Duke cries. "For what? For a speeding ticket?"

"I have here that he assaulted a police officer."

"What?" Duke roars. "Fine. Where do I pay bail?"

"Courthouse next door."

Before Duke walks out, I hear him call, "I'll be right back, Tanner. I'll look for you a good lawyer while I'm there."

Half an hour later, he comes back, and the officer lets me out of the cell. I have to sign some paperwork, and then, we are free to go. Somehow, in this whole process, Judd has disappeared. Probably a good thing because I worry what Duke would have done to him.

When we are safely inside Duke's truck, he says, "You want to tell me what's going on? Why am I bailing you out of jail?"

"Because I was arrested by the ex-husband of the woman I'm now dating."

He chews on his lip and slowly nods. "How about I buy you a beer?"

"This Judd guy sounds like a son-of-a-bitch," Duke says after I tell him the whole story.

"Yep," I say, taking a swig of my beer.

"What are you going to do?"

I shrug my shoulders. "What can I do? At the end of the day, this isn't my battle. It's Erin's."

"Do you think she will say something to him when you tell her what happened?"

"I don't know that I'm going to tell her."

His eyes go wide. "Why the hell wouldn't you tell her?"

"Because I'm not exactly innocent in this whole thing. If I would have kept my mouth shut, Judd probably would have just given me a ticket and walked away. But I took the bait and just had to engage."

"You think she would be mad at you?"

"Shit, I have no idea. But right now, I'm not trying to do anything to make her life any more difficult."

"And what if this asshole really doesn't drop the charges? You could end up doing some time for this."

"Guess I better find myself a good lawyer, huh?"

We both sit quietly for a moment before I say, "Thanks for coming to bail me out. I'll pay you back."

"Eh, don't worry about it. I figure I haven't bought you a birthday gift in twenty-five years. Maybe this will make up for that."

I laugh. "Getting married has turned you soft."

"Fuck, yes, it has. And I wouldn't have it any other way." He takes another drink. "You think Erin is *the one?*"

"Absolutely, but it's sure as shit not going to be easy to make it work."

"Look, Tanner, if Avery had wanted something easy, she sure as shit wouldn't have picked me. But you know what she tells me all the time?"

"What's that?"

"That the best things in life are never easy. No work, no reward."

Chapter Thirty-one

"**M**om, what do you want me to do with this box?" Alex asks. Chris is on a hunting trip with his dad, and things have been tense between Tanner and me for the past week, so he's staying at his place tonight. I'm not sure exactly why. When I ask him what's going on, he tells me nothing, but something is off. I thought we were doing much better, but maybe not. I'm half-expecting him to dump me any minute because he can't deal with all my drama, so until then, I am trying to keep myself busy... hence us cleaning out the attic.

I haven't been up here in forever. Pretty sure it was the day that we moved in—or soon after. I took all of the junk that I didn't want to deal with and shoved it up here. I figure after a year, it's time for me to go through some of it and downsize.

Looking at the box Alex is holding, I see that it's labeled ERIN'S JOURNALS.

"Oh my gosh!" I say. "I haven't seen these in forever!"

I take the box out of his hands and blow the dust off the top before opening it up.

"When are those from?" Alex asks.

"Oh, geez," I think out loud. "I started journaling when I was in late middle school or early high school? And I probably kept doing it through around the time that you were born."

He looks completely confused. "What did you write about? Was your life that exciting that you had to document it?"

After a hard eyeroll, I look at him. "You know, I'm not always as boring as you think I am."

"Sorry. I just can't imagine writing down that much of my life."

Cracking open one of the journals, I say, "I guess I was always better at writing things down than talking about them."

When he sees me sit down on the floor and start to read one of the books, he asks, "Can I go take a break? Maybe take Joey outside? I promise to keep an eye on him."

Without removing my eyes from the pages, I mutter, "Go for it."

An hour later, I've busted open a bottle of wine and am now reading all my journals while sitting on the couch next to Charlie. The boys have been outside this whole time. I think they are worried that if they dare to come inside, I'll put them back to work.

Reading through everything, I can see how much I've changed over the years. My high school entries are so much more fun and vivacious.

September 20th:

That cute guy, Judd asked me out again today. He's nice enough, but I think maybe he's *too* nice. I can tell that he's the type of guy you bring home to meet your parents before he slaps a ring on your finger. I'm not sure I'm ready for all that. Especially since just a couple days ago, I was making out with Tommy Markell at his party. The thing with Tommy isn't going anywhere, though. He tried to tell me he didn't like the way I dressed, so I told him to fuck off.

Besides, I only have half a year left until I graduate and can leave this small town in my dust. I still have no idea what I want to do, but I sure as shit know I don't want to stay here. I plan on doing something with my life.

But this Judd guy is cute, I guess. Maybe just one date wouldn't hurt.

I take a bit gulp of wine. Oh, sweet, naïve little Erin. You have no idea what you're getting into.

Another entry is from a couple years later.

June 2nd:

I don't know how much more of this I can take. Judd is driving me absolutely crazy. He keeps trying to change everything about me. He doesn't like my mouth or the way that I dress. He tells me

I'm a huge flirt with every guy I come in contact with.

I'm going to end it. I've been stuck here for longer than I wanted to, and it's time I really start my life. Deep down, Judd is a good guy, but I don't think that he's the right guy for me.

Wish me luck.

Two days later...

June 4ᵗʰ:

I'm pregnant. I'm fucking pregnant. How did this happen? Okay, I KNOW how this happened. But we were always careful. When I told Judd, he was the happiest I'd ever seen him. It's like it never dawned on him that we are still just kids with our whole lives ahead of us. I guess having a kid doesn't affect his plans on becoming a cop. But it sure as hell affects me.

When I told him, he said, "We should get married." What an absolutely grand proposal. I feel like I'm straight out of a romantic movie.

I keep telling myself that maybe it won't be that bad. Maybe a baby will help Judd chill out a little bit and find his softer side. I guess I can still do some painting and some writing and maybe try to build a portfolio that one day, I can use to get a good job.

I know they say that you will love the baby inside of you. And I guess part of me already does. But part of me feels like I have some sort of alien inside me. It no longer feels like my body. I hope that feeling goes away because I don't want to resent this kid before it even comes out.

Listen to me. I already sound like a terrible mother.

What the hell am I going to do?

The entries get more and more infrequent. I went from journaling every single day to maybe once every few months.

September 18th:

I felt the baby move for the first time today. Up until this point, I have been entirely unsure about this whole thing. As crazy as it sounds, those few little fluttery kicks were enough to make me realize how much I already love this baby. Judd has gotten better, and things have actually been going really well. It's like having a baby has softened him.

But no matter what, I know that it will be this kid and I against the world. Whether Judd is around or not, I will love and protect this baby with my life. It may have taken a few months for me to get my head out of my ass, but now that I'm here, I finally get it. I understand that it's my job to not only make sure this kid is loved but make sure they can take on anything that comes their way. I'll be the pillar of strength for them.

Next week, we get to find out what the sex is. I don't care what it is as long as it's healthy, but I secretly am hoping for a boy. I've always heard that daughters have an incredible bond with their dad while boys have the same with their mom. Plus, boys are supposed to be easier, right? I'm not sure I'm ready for all the girl

hormones. Give me boy problems any day of the week.

No matter what, I know one thing for sure, I will love this kid with every fiber of my being.

I already do.

When I finish reading that one, tears fill my eyes. I still remember the day that I felt each of my boys move for the first time. It was always the highlight of my pregnancies. And with each one, I always had the same feeling. I knew that I would love my kids with every single part of me. The day that I first felt Chris move, I decided that everything I did from then on would be for my kids. I would make sure that not only were they taken care of, but they were happy.

I felt like I failed them when Judd and I got divorced. I thought that I ruined their childhood and that they were going to need boatloads of therapy. Honestly, they handled it pretty well. It was me who could probably have used some therapy.

All those years ago, I vowed to make sure my kids were ready to take on anything the world would throw at them. Instead, I have been sheltering them from almost everything. Instead of showing them how to deal with things, I pretend everything is fine and sweep it under the rug.

Who is that helping?

I read another entry from a couple years later.

May 15th:

Judd has finally finished his time at the academy. I'm hoping that now that he doesn't

have the stress, he will be in a better mood. There are some times when he won't say a kind word to me for days. It's hard living with someone who only points out your flaws. Ever since I gave birth to Chris, all Judd talks about is my weight. I'm trying to lose it, but I'm just so tired all the time. When I try to talk to him about it, he just tells me I don't understand the stress that he's under.

I'm pretty sure I do considering I'm the one who has been working while he finishes school. My dad has been watching Chris since Judd says he's too busy studying to worry about babysitting. Can it be considered babysitting when it's your own kid?

I get so upset and feel like I'm ten seconds away from walking out the door. But then, Judd comes home with flowers or wants to have a picnic with Chris and I, and somehow, I just let it all go. How long am I going to continue to put up with it? How long am I going to stay with someone who clearly doesn't care about me?

I hear him coming through the front door. The way he threw his bag down and kicked off his boots lets me know that tonight isn't going to be a good one. He's going to be in a mood again, and I'll end up going to bed alone.

What the hell has happened to my life?

Now, I'm practically sobbing. With each entry I read, I can feel the younger me slowly losing myself. That once strong woman has turned into someone completely different. I'm so angry with Judd, but more so, I put the blame on myself. I should have never let him take as much from me as he did.

And I'm still letting him take things from me. Time and time again.

I'm letting a guy who treated me like shit dictate my relationship with a guy who treats me like a queen. What the hell is wrong with me?

When will enough be enough?

I pack up all the journals and take them back to the attic and spot another tote labeled **Erin's stories.**

No fucking way.

The box comes back downstairs with me, and I start looking through them. Back in the day, I used to want to write books. Writing romance was the dream, but Judd would tell me that it would embarrass him if I ever tried to publish something like that. I dabbled with a few thriller stories but never got very far. Pulling out the first notebook, I start reading a very rough draft of a love story that I wrote damn near ten years ago.

It's nowhere near a finished story, but the bones of it are good.

Just when I'm getting to a good part, I'm startled when Chris busts through the door.

"What are you doing here?" I ask. "I thought your dad was bringing you home tomorrow."

"We got in an argument. I told him I wanted to go home, and he told me to walk."

He goes to walk off to his room, but I have about a hundred questions. "Whoa, whoa, whoa. Stop right there. Get over here and tell me what happened."

"It doesn't matter," he mumbles.

"Of course it matters. Why would you say that?"

He finally looks at me. With a raised voice, he says, "Because you won't do anything about it!"

"Okay, I feel like you're on step number ten, and I'm back on step number one. Why are you mad at me?"

He pushes his hair out of his face. "Because you let him walk all over you."

His words hit me like a punch in the gut. "I... I don't... " I stammer over my words.

"You may think that I am just a kid, but that doesn't mean I don't notice things. I hear all the mean things he says to you."

Tears sting my eyes. "I never wanted you to hear any of that. That's why I do my best to keep everything civil."

"Well, no offense, Mom, but you're doing a shit job. Because not only is he being awful to you, but he's starting to take it out on Tanner."

"What are you talking about?"

"He didn't tell you that he pulled Tanner over and arrested him? Because he sure as heck was bragging about it to his buddies all day. He pulled him over for speeding and then charged him with assaulting a police officer."

"What?" I practically yell. "Why wouldn't Tanner tell me?"

"Would it have done any good? Or would you keep looking the other way?"

I feel like I'm going to vomit. I guess that's a pretty damn good reason as to why Tanner has been acting so weird lately.

"Mom, we like Tanner, and I think you do too, but you're letting dad run him right out of our lives. I got mad at him and told him that I didn't like him talking about you or Tanner, and he started yelling. When I yelled back, he slapped me. I wanted to come home, but he told me to walk. So, I did."

"He slapped you?"

In this moment, my thirteen-year-old, who is now taller than me, looks like a scared little kid. I didn't keep my promise to protect my baby boy.

Grabbing my keys off the table, I say, "I need you to watch your brothers. I'll call and see if your grandpa can come over and hang out."

Storming out the front door, only one word keeps playing over and over again in my mind.

Enough.

Chapter Thirty-two

ERIN

On the drive, I call my dad and get him to come over and sit with the kids for a while. Of course, he jumped at the chance.

Ten minutes later, I pull into Judd's driveway. I don't wait before getting out of the car because I don't want to lose my nerve. As if the sky opened up just for me, it's pouring down rain as I walk to the door.

The pit that normally occupies my stomach anytime I have to deal with Judd is now replaced with white hot rage.

Banging on his door, I yell, "Judd, we need to talk. Now!"

He opens and looks me up and down. "What the hell, Erin? You look like a drowned rat."

"Did you slap our son?"

He crosses his arms over his chest. "Yes. He needs to learn some respect."

"Respect? What the fuck do you know about respect?" I spit.

"Glad to know your back to cussing like a sailor. You can take the girl out of the trailer park but... well, you know the rest."

"Enough!" I yell. "I'm done with you and your bullshit."

"Is that right?"

Trying to push down any tears that may be struggling to make their way to the surface, I say, "For years, I have put up with you. I have taken the brunt of your insults, and I have tried to keep the peace, but I'm done."

With every passing second that I look at Judd, I just get more and more angry. I want to punch him in his stupid face.

Not giving him any time to speak, I ask, "Did you really arrest my boyfriend?"

He laughs. The kind of laugh that a psychopath gives after hurting a puppy. "Come on, Erin. I was just having some fun with him."

Moving closer to him, I say, "Let me tell you how this is going to go. You're going to drop ALL of the charges against Tanner. You are going to be nice to him in passing. When you pick up the kids, you will smile and wave to both of us without saying one negative word, and then, you will leave. You will never lay a finger on any of our kids ever again. And unless it involves our children, you will stay the fuck out of my life from now on."

With a little smirk, he asks, "And what if I say no to all of that?"

I pull out my phone and hold it up. "Do you know what I have on here, Judd? Every negative word you've ever spoken to me. Every nasty text message. Every angry voicemail. I'm sure a judge would be very eager to hear how to speak to me, and even more eager to hear that you slapped our son who just wanted you to stop talking bad about his mom. If you don't play by *my* rules from here on out, I will take you to court. I will file for sole custody of the kids, and I will win. And unlike you, when I say it, it isn't some empty threat. I mean every word. So go ahead. Try me."

We stand there staring at each other for a few moments before Judd says, "Just where exactly did you suddenly get your big brass balls from?"

"Judd, you have known me for over fifteen years now. What's the one thing in this world you don't mess with? My kids. So, I guess I should really be thanking you. If you wouldn't have hit Chris, I'd still be sitting at home, half scared of you, and keeping my mouth shut."

"Let's say you did take me to court. Do you really think you could raise three boys by yourself?"

Now, it's my turn to smile. "Who said I would be doing it by myself?"

"You really trust *that* guy to help you with three boys? He's going to run out faster than I don't know what."

"Judd, he hasn't run off yet, and he's been put through the ringer." I say the words, and I hope to God they are still true. I hope that he's still willing to give this a shot. "Tanner has never wanted to take your place. He isn't trying to play daddy. But he's another person to care about our kids. Just like Mary Louise is. How would you feel if I treated her like trash?"

He stands quietly for a moment before saying, "I wouldn't let that happen."

"Well, guess what, buddy? I'm *done* letting it happen with Tanner. So, the ball is in your court. Either get over yourself, or we can go to court and let them handle this. Your choice."

Before he can actually respond, I storm out the door. I pull out of his driveway so fast that my tires squeal. I'm halfway down the street before I have to pull over. My tears are flowing so hard that I can barely see out of the windshield.

As soon as the car is stopped, I let out the loudest scream that I can. It feels like fifteen years of bad energy is rushing out of my body. No longer will I let that man dictate a single thing that I do.

My tears are not ones filled with sorrow but ones filled with liberation. I feel like for once in my life, I'm doing things on my own terms.

And I'm just getting started.

In no hurry to go home, I drive around for a while once I've contained my tears. I want to go talk to Tanner, but I have no idea what I want to say yet. I'm not sure quite how to convey how much of an idiot I've been this whole time.

I end up in the town square. Maple Oaks may be small, but I hardly ever come into the heart of it. The kids' school is on the outskirts of town, and when I need groceries, I typically hit up Walmart or

Costco. I never really have a reason to come down here.

Some new shops have gone in, and I drive slowly past to see what they are. One catches my eye, and I immediately park.

Tattoos.

Running on nothing but adrenaline and impulse, I head straight inside. A big muscly guy with a handlebar mustache and a cobweb tattoo on his neck comes out to greet me. He looks me up and down because I'm still half soaked.

"You okay, Miss?" He asks, looking a bit worried.

"I'm great. I'm here to get a tattoo."

"Do you know what you want?"

I nod, and he takes me back to one of the rooms. I explain to him what I want to get and where I want it, and he gives me a price.

"Sounds good to me," I tell him.

With every stab of the tattoo gun on my wrist, I feel like I'm letting go of another thing I've held onto for far too long. For too long, I have been made a victim, but no more.

As the word comes into view on my wrist, tears sting my eyes once again.

Enough.

The word has so many meanings for me now.

Enough of the bullshit that I've endured.

Enough of letting my past get in the way of happiness.

And most of all, I am enough.

The tattoo artist, who I learned is named Jim, sees my emotions and hands me a tissue. "Do you need to take a break?"

"No, I'm fine," I tell him.

There's a kindness in his eyes like he understands the deeper meaning behind this tattoo. He gets back to work but says, "It'll be alright, darlin'. It always is."

When it's finished, I tip him $100 and give him a hug. I don't know this man from Adam, but I appreciate his kind words.

As I'm leaving the shop, I'm not watching where I'm going, and I run smack dab into Tanner's mom.

What are the fucking odds?

"Oh, Tammy, I'm so sorry," I tell her.

"Geez, Erin. Are you in a hurry?"

"Something like that."

"I'm surprised you're not with my son," she says with a hint of sarcasm.

That *don't give a damn* attitude still courses through my veins, and I have absolutely no control over what my mouth does at the moment, so I say, "Tammy, look, you may hate me. You may think I'm not good enough for your son, and that's fine. But let me tell you something—I just threatened to take my ex back to court if he didn't get out of my business with Tanner. I am just about tired of people fucking with us, and I know you're his mother, so I'm going to try to say this as nicely as I can. I will do anything for your son. He has pulled me out of such a dark place, and I will never be able to repay him for that. But you better believe I'm going to try. You can hate me. You can try to push me away all you want, but I'm not going anywhere. So, you better get used to it."

I wish I had a microphone to drop as I walk away. That would really come in handy tonight.

As I get back into my car, I realize that I'm making a whole lot of assumptions about Tanner and me sticking together through it all, but as far as I know, he's still not thrilled with me. What if he doesn't want to make it work? What if he's done with all the drama?

Not wanting to wait a minute more to find some answers, I drive to his house.

Chapter Thirty-three

TANNER

A pounding on my front door wakes me from the nap I was taking on the couch. They way they are banging on it makes me question if it's the cops. Probably Judd coming to haul me away.

Again.

When I swing open the door, I see Erin standing there, drenched from the rain. And she looks like you've been crying.

"Erin? Are you okay?"

She nods. "Can we talk?"

"Of course. Come on in. Do you want me to get you some dry clothes?"

She starts pacing. "No, I'm okay. I need to say some things to you."

"Alright, I'm listening." I walk over to the open kitchen and get some water boiling on the stove.

She follows me and starts talking as she does it. "Why didn't you tell me Judd arrested you?"

That makes me stop cold. "I thought you'd be mad."

"At you?"

I nod.

"Tanner, I'm not mad at you at all. In fact, I need to apologize to you."

"For what?"

She pushes away a strand of hair that was stuck to her face. "Okay, let me start from the beginning. Buckle up because it's going to be a bumpy ride."

Without pausing for even a second, she jumps right in. "Today, I found all these old journals of mine, and I realize just how much Judd has taken from me over the years. I used to be a totally different person. I thought that person was gone for good, but then, I met you, and she started to come back. Through a very chaotic list of events today—one that includes Judd putting his hands on my child—"

"Wait, what?" I interrupt.

"Yeah. I got so mad, and I just went over, and I went off on Judd. Told him that he needs to get over himself, or I was going to fight him for sole custody of the kids. Demanded that he drop the charges against you. I told him he needs to leave you alone because I'm in love with you, and you're not going anywhere. At least I hope you're not."

Before I can answer, she keeps going. "God, it felt so good to just let him have it. I let out everything that I've been holding in for so long. You should have seen it. It was a fucking work of art. Speaking of works of art." She points to some cling wrap covering her wrist. "I got a tattoo! A tattoo! Me!"

I take her wrist and read what it says.

Enough.

"I love it," I tell her.

"I mean it, Tanner. I've had enough of all of that. I'm so sorry I've put you through all of this, but I promise you will never have to miss another soccer game. I will never put Judd before you again."

Tears now stream down her cheeks. "I just hope it's not too late. If I were you, I would be over all of this by now."

I walk over to where she stands. Reaching my hands under her ass, I lift her up and set her on the counter. Lightly rubbing my thumb across her cheek, I say, "I meant it when I said I'm not going anywhere. Erin, as far as I'm concerned, you're my forever. I want to go to sleep with you every night and wake up with you every morning. I want to be the only guy that you kiss for the rest of your life. I want to be another person that your kids can depend on. I'm sorry I have been distant lately. I just felt bad for not telling you about the whole arrest thing. I didn't want to add more stress, but I'd feel guilty every time I was around you because it felt like I was being dishonest. But I promise no more secrets."

"No more secrets," she agrees as I slowly press my lips to hers.

She pulls back and looks at me. "While we are being honest, I think I should tell you that I also went off on your mom tonight."

"Huh?"

She tells me about how she ran into my mom—literally—and then gave her a piece of her mind.

When she's done, I ask, "Do you know how much I love you?"

She nods. "I think I have a pretty good idea."

This time, she initiates the kiss. It doesn't take long for it to turn hot and heavy. I interrupt to ask, "Do we need to get back to your place with the kids?"

She shakes her head. "My dad has them at the moment. We've got some time."

As I lead her to the bedroom, I say, "Babygirl, we've got forever."

Chapter Thirty-four

ERIN

"Okay, that man of yours is really something else," Gina tells me as she watches Tanner run around the yard having a NERF gun fight with all the kids.

"I know," I tell her as I finish writing HAPPY BIRTHDAY, JOEY in icing on the cake on the table in front of me. "He's incredible. He manages to still travel for work, help the kids with their homework, play outside with them, help me with dinner, and then still give me orgasms every night."

Gina laughs. "It's good to see you so happy. Wasn't sure if we would ever see it again."

"I guess I should thank you guys for making me get up there and sing karaoke. One of the best things I've ever done."

She shrugs her shoulders. "Eh, just invite us to the wedding. When is that going to be, by the way?"

"Pssh. You're way ahead of us. Right now, we are just living in bliss—and sin. I'm sure it'll happen eventually, but we are in no hurry."

"Have you guys talked about more kids?"

Now, it's my turn to shrug. "Tanner says he's fine without having any of his own, but I almost think it would be doing a world a disservice not even to try to have a baby with his blue eyes. We'll see if it happens."

Someone calls Gina's name, and she walks off to see what she wants. Meanwhile, my eyes are glued to Tanner. I watch as he takes care of Joey who looks like he just skinned his knee. I'm constantly in awe of how this man loves my kids as his own.

And to think I almost let it all go.

After I had the altercation with Judd, he backed off. And dropped the charges against Tanner. He isn't exactly pleasant toward us—more like he just picks up and drops the kids off without saying a word. He doesn't even come to the door anymore.

Fine by me.

He and Mary Louise are now expecting a baby, so I guess he's got his hands full with that.

Tanner's mom finally came around. She apologized for her behavior, and now, the kids, Tanner, and I all have dinner with her and Rob every couple of weeks.

Tanner sees me smiling at him and comes over to see what I'm doing. "Hey, beautiful," he greets.

"Hey, baby."

"The cake looks great!" He says it with a ton of enthusiasm, but I know it looks like one of those *nailed it* videos you see on the internet. It's not pretty.

I laugh. "Liar. Let's just hope it tastes good."

He says, "Hey, your dad offered to take the boys camping tonight. I told him I'd talk to you, but I figured you could get some writing done if you want."

Have I mentioned I now have a man who encourages me to write those romance novels? I'm well on my way to finishing my first one officially.

"Do you know how wonderful you are?" I ask.

He nods. "I've been told that many times."

Playfully, I smack him in the shoulder. "Well, don't get cocky. But to answer your question, I don't care if the boys go with my dad, but I don't know if I'll do any writing."

"Why not? Everything okay?"

Leaning in close, I say, "Well, I'm having trouble with this one sexy scene. I just can't get the details right. I was thinking maybe you could help me act it out. You know... for research purposes."

"Babygirl, by the time I get done with you, you're going to be able to finish the whole damn book."

The end.

Want a sexy epilogue for Tanner and Erin?

Sign up for my newsletter to get your copy here!

https://dl.bookfunnel.com/7fyg9jehgt

What's next?

Ready to meet the final Samson brother? Devon is arriving Fall 2023! Grab your copy here! https://www.amazon.com/gp/product/B0C7WGF 596

Also By Stephanie Renee

<u>The Constant Series</u>

A Constant Surprise

A Constant Reminder

A Constant Love

A Constant Christmas

<u>Spin-offs</u>

Seeing Red

Aces Wild

<u>The Grady Series</u>

All the Right Things

All the Right Reasons

All the Right Choices

All the Right Moves

All the Right Moments

All the Right Ideas

All the Right Memories

The Samson Boys

Duke's Redemption
Tanner's Forever
Devon's Deal (Coming Fall 2023)

Standalone Books

Beauty and the Boss Man

The House Always Wins
Have a Little Faith (Part of the Cinnamon Roll Saviors Collab)